'What secrets

'I could tell you i
Brendan said.

Terri waited hopefully for more but it did not come.

'I answered your questions. I thought you might be polite enough to return the compliment.'

'Oh, I'm polite enough, Miss Butler, when the necessity arises . . .'

Dear Reader

Here we are once again at the end of the year...looking forward to Christmas and to the delightful surprises the new year holds. During the festivities, though, make sure you let Mills & Boon help you to enjoy a few precious hours of escape. For, with our latest selection of books, you can meet the men of your dreams and travel to far-away places—without leaving the comfort of your own fireside!

Till next month,

The Editor

Lilian Peake grew up in Essex. Her first job was working for a writer of mystery stories. Subsequently, she became a journalist on a provincial newspaper, then moved to a trade magazine and reported on fashion. Later, she took on an advice column on a women's magazine. She began writing romances because she loves happy endings! She lives near Oxford, England, with her husband, a retired college principal. They have two sons and a daughter. Her hobbies are walking, reading and listening to classical music.

Recent titles by the same author:

NO PROMISE OF LOVE

INNOCENT DECEIVER

BY

LILIAN PEAKE

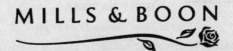

MILLS & BOON

MILLS & BOON LIMITED
ETON HOUSE, 18-24 PARADISE ROAD
RICHMOND, SURREY TW9 1SR

*All the characters in this book have no existence outside the imagination
of the Author, and have no relation whatsoever to anyone bearing the
same name or names. They are not even distantly inspired by any
individual known or unknown to the Author, and all the incidents are
pure invention.*

*MILLS & BOON and the Rose Device
are trademarks of the publisher.*

*First published in Great Britain 1994
by Mills & Boon Limited*

© Lilian Peake 1994

*Australian copyright 1994   Philippine copyright 1994
This edition 1994*

ISBN 0 263 78768 0

*Set in Times Roman 10 on 11 pt.
01-9412-57646 C*

Made and printed in Great Britain

CHAPTER ONE

HELPING her employer from the rear seat of the car, Terri placed a walking stick in the pale, veined hand that clutched it as if it were an extension of itself.

Moving to the lady's side, she hooked her arm through the one that was crooked to receive it, guiding the upright and determined figure across the bumpy gravel and up the stone steps to the porticoed entrance door.

'Don't support me,' said the lady testily, 'as if I were about to go sprawling on the ground. I may be old, my dear, but I'm not an ancient monument that needs propping up. When you've been here three months instead of just three weeks, you'll know that I need a certain amount of physical help, but *no more*, do you understand?'

'I'm certainly learning, Mrs Stewart,' Terri answered with a smile. 'If you'll tell me whenever I start treating you as if you were an *old* eighty-five-year-old, instead of the *young* eighty-five-year-old that you are, I shall learn all the quicker.'

'I'll have no impudence from you, young woman,' said Mrs Stewart, but a smile softened her words.

The heavy door to the great stone residence swung open and a grey-haired man who, like his employer, looked young for his age smiled and bowed with old-world charm, taking over from Terri.

'Welcome home, Mrs Stewart,' said the man.

'I've only been to town, Harvey,' his employer exclaimed with an asperity for which he seemed to have been waiting, since he smiled again, 'not on a trip around the world! And you, young lady——' she half turned to

Terri '—are now free to take yourself off to wherever you go when I give you the time off that's your due.'

Terri hesitated, then asked boldly, 'The rowing boat that I've seen beached on the edge of the water whenever I've walked that way——'

'The one that bears my name—*Christiana*?'

'That's right.'

'It belongs to the Stewart family.'

'I guessed. I hope you don't mind my asking, but would it be seaworthy?'

Mrs Stewart faced her. 'If you mean is it waterproof and safe to use, then I should hope it is. Why?'

'Well——' Terri's eyes grew dreamy '—it's just that the far shore looks so inviting I'd love to row over there and investigate.'

'Have you rowed before? You have? I asked because while you're working for me I'm responsible for your safety. Anyway——' a smile softened her rather austere features '—I've come to like you and your company too much, young woman, to lose you at this stage of my life.'

Terri smiled, hesitating for a couple of seconds. 'I've been in a boat with an outboard motor on the River Thames. Now and then I took over for a while.'

Mrs Stewart missed nothing. 'By your hesitation, I suspect you went with a boyfriend?' Terri turned her head away. 'Since you've been here, you've shown no signs of yearning for him. Would I be intruding if I asked whether he was no longer in your life?'

'There's no one now,' Terri answered and her employer nodded with apparent satisfaction.

Turning to Harvey, Christiana Stewart asked, 'Is it in a usable condition?'

'The boat, ma'am? It certainly is. Whenever Mr Brendan comes, he's down there and in it before you can say Santa Claus. It's not just a rowing boat,' Harvey pointed out to Terri. 'It's got an outboard motor.'

'Excellent,' commented Mrs Stewart, then said to Terri, 'You're welcome to use it, but take care.' She began to move off, then halted, turning.

'Have you,' she asked, 'brought appropriate garments with you for such a trip? No? Then I suggest you go into my grandson's room, which is across the landing from yours, open his wardrobe and extract his waterproof jacket, and any other item of clothing that will keep you warm and dry.'

Terri frowned. 'But are you sure——?'

'Quite sure,' was the firm answer. 'He won't be needing them himself since he has no intention yet, as far as I'm aware, of paying me a visit. They're few and far between, are Brendan's visits, and considering I brought him up——' A brisk shrug dismissed any self-pity that might be read into her words.

'There are times,' she went on, 'when he'll descend, completely without warning, but, considering that he is at the present time working in London, I cannot see how even my grandson, clever though he is, can be in two places at once.'

She transferred her attention to Terri. 'The next time we go into town, you must purchase some suitable outdoor clothing for yourself.'

'You're quite sure,' Terri pressed, 'that your grandson wouldn't mind?'

'What the eye doesn't see,' retorted Mrs Stewart, 'the heart doesn't grieve over. Oh, and if the resident hound follows you it's up to you whether or not you want a canine companion.' With slow steps she moved towards the parlour. 'Tea, Harvey, and pronto,' she said, with a crooked smile that knocked three decades off her age and made Harvey's ample frame quiver with amusement.

The small white Scottie dog bounced determinedly after Terri, ignoring her instructions to return to the house and to his owner.

'OK, dog,' Terri said, pleased to have him share her few hours of freedom, 'we're going for a sail, you and I.'

She half walked, half ran over the rocky shoreline towards the sweeping stretch of water. Her shoulder-length deep brown hair danced on the strong breeze. Her eyes, lit with anticipation, were as blue as the cloud-scattered sky. Her rounded cheeks were pink, her lips parted with the exhilaration of pitting her strength against the wind's.

The quilted jacket she had borrowed billowed over a high-necked grey sweater which formed a warm layer over a man's grey collared shirt.

Her jeans, however, were intended, no question, for the female form, and in her case revealed the slim but undoubtedly feminine hips and long, shapely legs. Strong shoes covered her hurrying feet, around which the dog now yapped and chided.

'Stop it, Snippet,' Terri reprimanded, at which the dog withdrew a little, sitting on his haunches, breathing hard, his tail waving madly as he watched her. 'Come on, stupid,' she addressed the boat, then the dog; 'help me reach the water.'

Snippet danced around unhelpfully while the boat, its oars stowed, moved co-operatively and she managed to ease it over the ridged rocks, wetting her shoes as she followed it, stepping high and quickly over its side.

'Here, Snippet,' she called, and the dog paddled and jumped, joining her with a flourish of salty water.

Standing, Terri steadied the boat with her feet, gazing around. In the semi-distance was the three-storeyed grey stone house belonging to her employer. To the other side of the inlet was a white-painted cottage whose exterior, in the three weeks she had been in the area, she had come to know well and which, along with all the other unknown excitements that lay across the other side, seemed to draw her strangely.

The slate-tiled roof of the cottage sloped steeply. Dormer windows pushed through, facing proudly across the bay, while the rear overlooked the rough terrain of the mountains. It stood alone—and lonely, Terri had come to believe—some distance from the line of similar, if slightly smaller cottages away to her left.

A lone figure, made tiny by distance, strode determinedly. Unable to determine whether the walker was man or woman, Terri was sure that that person, whoever it might be, would not, in such a broad and sweeping landscape, intrude upon her personal space.

A road led to the settlement, she knew that, and that person was taking it, but she herself had opted for the quicker, more exciting, if slightly more hazardous method of reaching it. Patting the deep pocket of the man-sized jacket she had borrowed, she felt her meagre provisions—a packet of sandwiches and a small bottle of water.

Clouds, white to grey, massed to the west, while overhead the sky was a clear blue. No rain, at least not for a while, she estimated, although how accurate her weather reading would prove after such a short residence in the place she did not know.

Firing the engine and setting the boat on its course, she dropped down on to the wooden seat, the dog seated forward, staring out, as if he were pilot and captain rolled into one.

Passing a rocky island, Terri gazed around again, giving a short sigh of pleasure. The figure she had spied making tracks for the settlement had paused and appeared to be fascinated by the sight of the small boat's bobbing passage.

Well, she thought, I suppose we're something moving and therefore interesting for an inhabitant to gaze at in this quiet landscape.

The bow edged towards the boulders and stones that sprawled across the sloping beach. The popping of the engine died away. Terri jumped out, splashing a little, and Snippet followed, making for dry land, shaking himself and nosing around.

Hauling the boat above the water mark, Terri secured its mooring rope to a post which someone, no doubt in the distant past, had thoughtfully hammered into the grassy bank.

The white cottage drew her and as she walked towards it something in her responded to its solitude and isolation. An intense excitement gripped her.

'You want to write stories?' her sister Madge, a magazine fiction editor, had queried over lunch the day before Terri had left London for the job she had been offered in far-away—or so it had seemed at the time—Scotland. 'The kind I might accept for publication in my fiction slot? Think you've got the stamina to write a long one for serialisation? Have a try, if you like, or opt for a short length. It's up to you.'

How her sister's words had thrilled her, boosting her confidence that she had at least that one book inside her that some people alleged everyone possessed.

'So,' Madge had said, 'go up there, sister mine, and get your brain working on some ideas.' Fleetingly her hand had covered Terri's. 'I have to say that, although you are my little sister, you do seem to know how to write. And I don't just mean the school essays you used to write for English homework and for which you were consistently awarded top grade.'

Terri had coloured with pleasure. It wasn't often that she received any kind of praise from her sister. And for Madge to have remembered her school reports—she couldn't believe her luck.

'And,' Madge had continued, finding her credit card with which to settle the lunch bill, 'along with that creative ability you've had since you were a little kid, you actually had the brains to get high grades in the science subjects you took in your school-leaving exams. So go for it, kid, eh?'

'You know,' Terri had commented with a smile, 'I'm actually beginning to be glad that my old job closed down on me. Glad, too, I was offered the one I'm just about to take up.'

'All you have to do now,' Madge had told her, 'is to use your eyes and your ears, not to mention your imagination, and discover something—and I don't mean just any old thing—to write about. And once you've got an idea, tell no one or it will go. And remember to keep in touch, won't you?'

'Thanks a million, Madge. For the encouragement, I mean.' Filled with excitement at the prospect, Terri had hugged her big sister as they had parted.

All this, Terri thought now, letting the ambience of the place, the brooding nature of the environment, the hills and the loneliness, soak into her, could be exactly what I'm looking for. Her mind flashed up a vision of her name, not at the foot of the page as a mere byline, but *above* the title and the introductory blurb.

Heartbeats speeding up, she gazed through a window. A bare stone floor was covered here and there by woven rugs. The room appeared to contain a primitive oven, a wooden table and two or three chairs.

Moving round the building with Snippet at her heels, she discovered another window. This time the room she stared into seemed just a little more welcoming. Two sofas faced each other, standing each side of a black stove, its doors closed tightly, its interior empty of fuel and warmth.

To one side stood a plain wooden dining-table, and two or three dining-chairs. As she stared in through the glass, a tall male figure seemed to materialise in the doorway to the room. Her heart jolted, then bounded, a *frisson* of something curiously like fear passing through her. She had been certain that the place was empty. Even

as she gazed, the shadowy figure melted away and she
knew then that it was her imagination that had supplied
the strange apparition.

Quelling the shiver that took hold of her at the strange
phenomenon, she decided not to linger, but to get on
with exploring the area. At the rear of the cottage, she
gazed up at the mountain, a rough and rugged backdrop
to the settlement that lay away to her left, while misty
hills stretched into the distance, massive clouds rising
above them all.

For a few minutes she stood, absorbing the atmosphere, trying to form a mental picture to help her remember everything for her notes later. She was glad then
that she had remembered to bring a notebook and pencil.
If she were really to become a writer, she reminded
herself, those pieces of equipment, elementary but in-
dispensable, were an absolute 'must'.

'Come on, Snippet,' she called, stepping down the
grassy bank and sitting beside the boat. Pulling out the
packet of sandwiches, she bit into one, breaking off a
piece and holding it out to the dog.

He took it eagerly, waiting for more, then, when they
had finished the packet between them, she took out the
bottle of water and drank, finding a discarded can and
pouring some water into it for him.

While Snippet happily occupied himself seeking out
fresh scents, Terri lay back on her hands, staring at the
sky and thinking about the story she intended to write.

It was Snippet's indignant barking that dragged her
from the sleep she had had no intention of allowing to
overtake her. Glancing round, she saw nothing unusual
or worrying, nor did there seem to be a human being in
sight. She settled back, determined this time to stay
awake.

She fought back to consciousness and struggled upright, looking with dismay at her clothing. A downpour
was soaking her, while Snippet, she noticed ruefully,

plainly possessing more common sense, was sheltering under the boat.

'Oh, heavens,' she groaned. Snippet's tail wagged madly, inviting her to join him. 'If only I could shrink to your size,' she commented ruefully, 'I would.'

The earlier blue of the sky had disappeared behind storm clouds, and the rain had become torrential. She scrambled to her feet as heavy drops battered her uncovered head and soaked her borrowed clothes, drenching every part of her.

Helplessly she gazed around...and her heart almost stopped. From only a few strides away, a tall figure, cloaked in a yellow rain cape, stared back at her.

'If you know what's good for you,' the person rapped out from the depths of the cape, 'you'll take shelter.'

She knew for certain then that the figure she had seen striding along that distant road had been male, and that it was he who was now looking at her as if she had crawled from under a boulder.

'Where?' Her voice quavered, still dazed with sleep. Was this a dream, and she was talking to a character in that dream? 'There's nowhere that I can see——'

'There's here.' With the sweep of an arm, he opened up the cape, inviting her to share its protection.

'But I——' Don't know you, she had been going to say. Yes, definitely a dream, she assured herself, and tried to make herself wake up.

'For God's sake forget convention,' the abrasive male voice declared. 'Unless you want to get drowned while lying on dry land? I'll introduce myself like the gentleman I am not when we're in dryer surroundings. Now will you come?'

Snippet shivered beneath the boat. Knowing that she would feel safer with him at her side, Terri scooped him up and carried him towards the man. The dog snarled and tried to jump from her arms, but the man took him, holding him firmly.

So it wasn't a dream, she decided, blinking away from her eyelashes raindrops that simply replaced themselves with others. Snippet wouldn't respond in such a way to a non-existent being.

Snippet sniffed and snuffled in the man's arms, his small body still stiff with tension. Then, miraculously, he relaxed, sniffing at Terri, too, as if making sure she was there.

The man's hard shoulder was behind her as his arm lifted to draw her more effectively into the cape's protection. Her pulses leapt, her heart hammered, and she knew that it was not only with fear at his sudden appearance, nor the very unguarded way in which she had accepted his invitation to join him. The mere touch of him did something to her reflexes, but she would not allow herself to dwell on the disturbing fact. His ribcage moved as his lungs expanded and contracted, and she felt with a curious certainty that she was as safe as if she had known the man all her life.

Except that something inside her was warning her that, no matter what those reflexes of hers might be telling her, this man was surely dangerous—if not to her person, then to her peace of mind. She was, it lectured, as if suddenly possessed of foresight, anything but safe where this man was concerned, and if she possessed even a grain of common sense she would snatch Snippet, take to her heels and return to base as fast as the boat would carry them.

But she stayed right there, within the circle of the stranger's arms, allowing him to guide her towards the solitary cottage that earlier had intrigued her so much.

Opening the door, he propelled her into what she had guessed was the kitchen, let Snippet down and turned to shake the rain cape, draping it over a coat-stand.

'It's v-very kind of y-you,' she stammered, trying in vain to control her shivering body, 'but I could have——'

'Couldn't you see the storm clouds?' he clipped. 'Why didn't you read the signs?'

'Even if I'd been awake,' she defended her indefensible stupidity, 'I couldn't have "read" any kind of cloud in this part of the world. I come from the south——'

'You could have fooled me,' was his sarcastic rejoinder. His eyes did a quick survey of her appearance and a frown came and went. 'No offence meant,' he added, with a touch of sarcasm, 'but you resemble a bedraggled rabbit.'

He gestured towards a door which, she discovered, opened into the room in which she had spied the unlit black stove. Its doors were still closed, but now through its transparent windows she could see leaping flames, could smell the smoke of the logs that were burning brightly.

She turned to him, puzzled. 'When I looked through the windows earlier, the stove wasn't lit.'

'It was laid for instant use. I came in the back way and I put a match to the fire. I stared out at the rain, and saw you lying there. I couldn't believe my eyes. You didn't exactly look as if you had no more use for this world, so I had to investigate.'

'Just to make sure I was still breathing?'

He answered her smile with a quirk of his lips. 'Exactly.'

Unfastening the soaked jacket, she held out her hands gratefully to the stove's radiating warmth. As she basked in its glow, the shivering that had possessed her slowly died away. However, as hands started to ease the jacket from her shoulders, flicking away the wet strands of her hair and inadvertently trailing her neck as they did so, the shivering returned.

'The rest,' the man said as she turned to protest that his attentions were unnecessary, 'I leave to you.'

Snippet appeared to be completely at home, sniffing every corner and item of furniture. He seemed also to be drying faster and Terri could not suppress a smile as she watched the steam rising comically from his fur.

'Hi, dog,' said the man and Snippet actually wagged his tail. Traitor, Terri's reproachful stare reprimanded the animal, you should be crouching and snarling, protecting me.

'I'm sorry,' she said, feeling that maybe an apology was overdue, 'to have landed myself on you in this way. Thank you for coming to my rescue, but it's time we were——' She indicated the door.

'Have you looked outside?'

She hadn't, but she did so then and saw that the rain had, if anything, intensified. The outlook, she reflected, was gloomy, to put it mildly, the room itself having darkened, creating shadows where well-defined outlines had been before.

It was then that she began to be afraid. If this—this creepy feeling was what researching for a story involved—the hands-on approach, didn't they call it, experiencing things at first hand?—then why in heaven's name was it her ambition to be a writer?

Hadn't she, her reason lectured, broken all the rules that common sense dictated, unthinkingly following the lead of her imagination? She had entered the house of a stranger, having made no effort to tell anyone where she was and taking heaven knew what risks by her thoughtless actions.

She looked at the man, seeking a glimmer of something, anything, to reassure her—in his demeanour, his expression, most of all in his eyes. Nothing was there except blankness. Then recognition dawned and a shock flashed through her.

This was surely the man she had seen as she'd gazed in through the window—the 'apparition' that had come and gone even as she had stared. The tempo of her heart increased, almost choking her. How could she have imagined this man? She had never seen him before in her whole life, so how could her mind, in league with her imagination, have possibly conjured up his image?

Her legs gave notice of their intention to sag and finally did so, depositing her in a crumpled heap on the hearth-rug at the stranger's feet.

There was a muffled exclamation and hands caught her under the armpits, hauling her up and against a hard expanse of chest. Her forehead rooted for the man's shoulder and his arms went round her shivering form. Some of his strength, she reasoned hazily, must have communicated itself to her as the shivering gradually lessened and died away.

At last her legs took over their rightful role and she lifted herself away from him. At once she missed the security of his solid frame and the curious sanctuary his hard body had offered.

'Thank you, and I'm sorry again,' she managed. 'I've never fainted in my life before and I——'

'You didn't faint.' His brisk manner helped her pull herself together far more effectively than sympathy would have done. 'You collapsed with——' He frowned again. 'I guess it was something akin to exhaustion. But it looked as if you'd seen a ghost.'

I had, I had, she almost cried, but shook her head instead.

'Will you tell me something?' he asked after a pause in which Snippet took Terri's place on the hearthrug, resting his nose on his paws and dropping off to sleep. 'How is it——?' He looked her over again and a frown pleated his brow which Terri felt an overwhelming and totally astonishing urge to lift her fingertips and press away.

'How is it,' he repeated, 'that we've never met in our lives before, yet here you are, wearing *my* jacket, *my* shirt——' he touched each item '—and *my* pullover? And who,' with heavy sarcasm, 'if I may be forgiven for asking, gave you permission to use *my* boat to get yourself and this hound across the inlet?'

CHAPTER TWO

FOR the second time that day, Terri's legs threatened to withdraw their services. She felt herself go cold. No wonder Snippet hadn't seen this man as an enemy. The man's own scent was on the clothes that *she* was wearing!

And hadn't Snippet sussed that out, she reflected, with his clever canine sense of smell, the moment this man had taken him over and held him?

'You're——' she swallowed a gasp '—*you* are Mrs Stewart's grandson?'

'I am Brendan Stewart,' he answered curtly. 'And you?'

'Mrs Stewart is my employer. I drive her around, make appointments for her socially, accompany her to various functions.' She frowned. 'If you're her grandson, how is it that you're living here——' the sweep of her arm encompassed the cottage, the land beyond '—and not occupying your room at your grandmother's house?'

His eyes darkened. 'I could tell you to get lost, to mind your own business.' His brows drew together. 'For a new-comer——' his eyes struck sparks '—you're asking a hell of a lot of intrusive questions. So you don't believe me, hmm?'

Do I? she asked herself. Yes, of course you believe him, her subconscious mind dictated. Then it told her why. On Mrs Stewart's grand piano stood a framed portrait of this man, plainly taken a few years before. Was the lapse of years, together with Mrs Stewart's habit of referring to him only as 'my grandson', the reason why it had taken her so long to notice the likeness and make the connection?

19

Before she could correct the impression that she doubted his word, he went on, 'How do I know that you're telling *me* the truth? What's your name?'

'Terri Butler. And you can come right over and check, if you want positive proof. Mrs Stewart—Mrs *Christiana* Stewart will testify as to my identity. Harvey, too.'

He smiled but it did not reach his eyes. 'You think that name-dropping will prove your case? Everybody knows everyone's name in these parts. There's a very efficient grapevine.'

'But it's true,' she cried. 'That is my name. And I *do* work for your grandmother. Even Snippet could tell you that.'

'OK, OK.' He looked down at the sleeping bundle. 'I wasn't aware that my grandmother owned a dog.'

'I'm not surprised you didn't know,' burst from her uncensored. 'Mrs Stewart was only saying today how long it's been since she's seen you. And she brought you up, too. You see, I even know that.'

His eyebrows arched, but he stayed silent.

'She's taken charge of Snippet until his real owner, a friend of hers, comes back from abroad.'

'Don't you think,' he commented, changing the subject abruptly, 'that you should change out of those wet clothes?'

Terri shook her head firmly. There was no way she would undress in front of this man. 'I haven't got anything to change into. All my belongings are over there at your grandmother's house.' She looked hopefully outside, but the rain was still pelting down.

'This'll go on for hours,' was his laconic, and faintly amused comment. 'If you stay around in these parts long enough, you'll discover that for yourself. And since you're already wearing my clothes, I'll lend you some others while those are drying.'

'Thanks, but no,' she responded.

He chose not to hear, returning with a checked shirt, a thick pullover and a pair of jeans, at which Terri frowned.

'These trousers are mine,' she said, looking down at the jeans she was wearing. 'I can't possibly wear yours.'

'For the life of me I can't see why not. You're already wearing so much that belongs to me, why make an exception of these?' He held the jeans high for her inspection. 'Clean, nearly new...' he eyed her slender hips '...somewhat large for you, maybe, like the other garments, but they'll serve a purpose while you wait for yours to dry.'

His words made sense and she reluctantly accepted the clothes. 'Is there somewhere I can change?' she asked stiffly.

A flicker of amusement crossed his eyes.

'A dying species...' His sarcasm surfaced again. 'A specimen of modern womanhood actually wanting privacy in order to divest herself of clothes? I feel an overwhelming urge to capture you and preserve you in a test-tube for posterity to study.'

Flushing deeply, she threw the clothes on to a chair.

'Thanks a lot. I don't care if it *is* pouring with rain; I'd rather endure that than stand here being insulted. Thank you for the hospitality. Snippet, come.'

He didn't come. Instead, he stirred, stretching, in no hurry to join her. She made for the door but a grip on her arm halted her before she could reach it, swinging her round. Snippet settled back to sleep.

Brendan Stewart looked inscrutably into Terri's flushed face.

'Through there,' he directed brusquely. 'Upstairs, first door on the right.' He bundled the clothes into her arms. 'The sleeping arrangements in this cottage are primitive. The bathroom facilities are only marginally more civilised. If I feel the need of luxury and a bit of cosseting, I go across to my grandmother's house. Here, there are two bedrooms but only one bed. The second bedroom is otherwise occupied.'

He must have caught the flash of fear in her eyes.

'And if your over-fertile imagination is busy filling that room with indescribable secrets——' how on earth did he know? she asked herself '—and even the results of dastardly deeds, then you can think again. It isn't even locked. But I warn you, neither a layman, in the professional sense of the word, nor even a *lay-woman*——' a hint of sensuality glinted in his eyes '—would discover anything to his—or her—advantage by putting his——'

'Or her?' Terri inserted.

'—*superior* nose in there. Make what you like of that, Miss Butler, but I do urge you to change into those dry things before you catch pneumonia. The dog's safe with me,' he added mockingly.

'Thank you for the reassurance, Mr Stewart,' she tossed back, 'but if my instinct for self-preservation surfaces in a situation like this, would it be sensible of me to suppress it?' With which she swept out, checked herself, then turned back. 'What "professional sense"?'

'Maybe I should have said "scientific". If you're asking what's my line, I'm a biochemist.'

'Um . . . I see.'

'Tell me, Miss Butler . . .' his voice was misleadingly soft ' . . . what do you see?'

'Well, your——' she gestured towards him '—your academic background, it sticks out around you like—like a hedgehog's prickles.' She made to go, but once again halted. 'Keeping ignoramuses like me, and people in general, at bay.'

She didn't wait to gauge his reaction. She pushed at a door, finding a roughly made-up bed and furniture which only a man who cared not a jot for material possessions, nor other people's critical evaluations of his actions, would tolerate.

Emerging flushed from her quick-change act, she found the bathroom, which, as he had claimed, was somewhat primitive, but contained reasonably modern fittings and, moreover, provided a perfectly acceptable standard of cleanliness.

Re-entering the living area, she saw that he had placed a clothes-airer in front of the closed-in fire. On this she draped the damp garments, hoping they wouldn't take long to dry.

Behind the closed doors, the fire roared with the fresh logs he had thrown on to it and for a few seconds, as she stared, the flames hypnotised her. She was experiencing the curious feeling of having come home, not just to physical warmth, but emotional, too. I could live here, not alone, but *with this man* ... The thought was so frightening in its intensity and implication, it jogged her out of her dream state and back to reality.

She felt his eyes on her. She hoped he couldn't read her thoughts, nor, in the fading light, see the colour wash over her cheeks.

'The jeans,' he commented drily, 'are full of promise. What happens if you let go of the waistband you're clutching as if your life depended on it?' His smile was genuine and Terri's heart did a somersault at the way his rather austere features came alive.

'That's something I'm not about to demonstrate,' she replied firmly.

'Here.' He took a length of string from a drawer and went to slot it through the loops, the backs of his hands brushing against her.

She tried to take the string and gripped his wrists to stop him. Their eyes clashed and did battle. It was hers that surrendered. The room and everything in it seemed to spin, her heart going with it. What was there about this man, she wondered agitatedly, that upset her equilibrium as no man had ever done before?

'If you would release my hands,' he said softly, 'I'll provide you with the physical, not to say moral support you seem to want.'

'Sorry,' came from her hoarsely and she complied at once.

His nearness unsettled her acutely. All his concentration was directed to the threading of the string, and Terri's eyes were drawn inexorably to him. There were things about him that she found she was noticing for the first time.

His hair was smooth and well-shaped, brushing down into a curved fringe, the style hinting at civilised living in a large metropolis where barbers paid attention to current styles adapted to an individual's wishes. The jaw curved its way to a resolute chin, the arched brows adding emphasis to the resolution in his steely grey eyes.

His lips told of an innate sensuality which, Terri was shocked to discover, caused a response inside her which she had sworn would lie dormant for the rest of her life. Never again, she had promised herself, would she let any man reach the woman in her. Consequently, the sense of panic she experienced at her system's response to his nearness appalled her, and she turned her head away from the faint but almost irresistible scent that was the essence of him and which had hung around all the garments she had borrowed from him.

'Not too tight?' he asked, stepping back.

'W-what?' Quickly she tried to hide the confusion her thoughts had created within her. 'Oh, yes, yes. I mean, no.' She tested the strength of the makeshift belt he had provided. 'Thank you. Very much.'

His eyes narrowed at her agitation and she hoped he had not guessed the reason for it.

The ticking clock on the mantelshelf warned her that several hours had passed since she had started across the inlet on her voyage of discovery.

'Your grandmother!' she exclaimed. 'She'll miss me; she'll begin to worry. Is there——?' Of course there wasn't. How could a telephone have been installed in such an out-of-the-way place when, judging by the old-fashioned oil lamp on the table, there wasn't even electricity laid on?

'A telephone?' He had read her thoughts. 'We're connected. And I've got a generator which supplies all the electricity I need, although I haven't got around yet to starting it up. While you were changing, I rang the house and told my grandmother that not only was I here, but that you were here safe and sound too. I told her not to expect you back before this storm has passed.'

'Which,' Terri remarked, her anxious glance out of the window confirming that the gale blew unabated, 'could mean some hours?'

'Morning, probably. So the sooner you reconcile yourself to spending the night with me——' a sardonic eyebrow flicked upwards, accompanying an equally sardonic smile '—the better.'

'If I thought you meant that literally, I'd——' Her glare towards the grim conditions outside finished the sentence.

'OK,' he countered crisply, 'let it drop.'

Terri's glance shot upwards furiously to entangle with his. 'You really do win first prize for putting women down. Do you have to keep making me feel small?' He did not answer and she added, 'You don't much like the female of the species, do you?' His expression gave nothing away. 'Well, I've got news for you, Mr Stewart, I don't like men much, either.'

'Quits,' he commented drily. 'We must get together some time and compare notes.'

Never, she thought, putting up her hands to smooth her damp tendrils. 'I hope you don't mind, but I used a towel in the bathroom to dry my hair.'

His shrug dismissed the subject and she wandered to the window. It was, if anything, raining even harder. Moreover, a wind had risen which threatened to increase any moment to gale force. Black, rain-bearing clouds made it seem as if night was not far away, although darkness, she had discovered since living so far north, normally descended late at that time of the year.

That story, she thought with a small smile. She was living it, wasn't she? She was living it here and now!

'Tell me something, Miss Butler.' He waited as she turned slowly to face him. 'You're young, attractive—don't try and deny it, you know you are. Why did you accept a job so far away from the kind of environment a woman of your age group usually opts for?' Hands in pockets, he moved closer. 'From what—or whom—are you running away?'

'Nothing, no one at all.' It had come out too quickly, too emphatically, Terri realised. 'I've got no secrets, nothing to hide,' she declared, then cursed herself for elaborating unnecessarily.

Secrets? Of course she had. I'm researching for a book I want to write... I'm absorbing everything around me... thinking out a plot... weaving it into the wild country all around. And nothing to hide? It came to her from nowhere that whatever else she did she mustn't tell this man—oddly suspicious of her presence as he seemed to be—a single thing about her sister's offer, the advice she'd been given to, as it were, get her nose to the ground and scent out something, anything, to write about.

Anyway, she decided, even if she told him, he would laugh, be sarcastic, dismiss the whole idea in his sardonic way. And, newcomer to the art of writing as she was, such cynical criticism would destroy her confidence and kill the whole idea stone-dead.

His eyebrows lifted, which could only mean that he hadn't believed her denial. So she would tell him the plain, unvarnished truth.

'I lost my job,' she told him. 'For a long time I looked for another. Your grandmother liked me enough to offer me this one. I was only too glad to accept.'

'So...' his narrowed eyes conveyed the fact that he didn't completely believe her '...no heartbreak? No man walking out?'

Her shoulders lifted and fell. She went to the hearth-rug and lifted Snippet to one side, sinking down on to the rug and occupying his place in front of the fire.

'I had a boyfriend. He wanted to get really serious. I didn't. We quarrelled. We parted.' She lifted her head. 'That's all. He did try to get me to change my mind, but I wouldn't. He took it badly, but accepted it in the end.'

Brendan nodded, giving no indication as to whether or not he had accepted her explanation.

'You asked me to bare my soul and I did. Fair's fair.' Her eyes challenged his. 'I could ask you what—or whom—you're running away from.'

His jaw hardened and she knew that she had over-stepped the mark. None the less, she pressed on. 'Why do you have this little hideaway so far from civilisation? What secrets have *you* got that you don't want the world to know?'

'I could tell you it's none of your business.'

She waited hopefully for more but it did not come. 'Which you now have. Sorry.'

He gazed steadily down at her. She supposed she should have known better than to goad him. What irritated her most was that he was quite right. It was none of her business. All the same, she felt the need to justify her probing.

'I answered your questions without reservation. I just thought you might be polite enough to return the compliment.'

'Oh, I'm polite enough, Miss Butler, when the necessity arises.' It was to be her only answer.

The dog rose and padded to the entrance, snuffling at the ground. 'He wants out,' Terri said and scrambled up, making for the door.

Brendan reached it first, letting Snippet through. Then, pulling on a jacket and putting up its hood, he exited quickly before the gale could force its way into the room.

In no time, Snippet was back, his fur wet through, which was not surprising, Terri reflected, since a glance out had told her how heavily it was raining. She began to despair of ever getting back across the inlet.

She took the towel that had been used before and rubbed a grateful Snippet down. He shook himself again and made a beeline for the hearthrug, sitting on it, panting.

Brendan returned, shedding his outerwear and hanging it to dry.

Terri watched him and said hopefully, 'I know it's a long way to go on foot by road, but if you could give me a lift——'

'My car's being serviced. I left it in the town on arrival this morning, then walked here.'

'I saw you in the distance. And,' Terri was unable to resist adding, 'I saw the way you watched me row over here.'

He nodded. 'I couldn't believe my eyes. *My* boat, *my* clothes, all purloined by a strange female and a strange dog.' He smiled and once again her heart leapt in response. 'Then, to see said female and dog snooping around *my* cottage, it was enough to make any sane individual doubt what his eyes were telling him.' The smile faded. 'What were you after?'

'Why do you keep trying to cast me in the role of petty criminal?' she protested, feeling more than ever that she was the heroine of her own as yet unwritten story. 'It was pure curiosity, nothing else. And if you could see so clearly when you were so far away, you must have been using binoculars.'

'Ten out of ten, Miss Butler, for such an accurate assumption.'

'So if you're innocent of any intrigue, why do you spy on people in such an underhand way?'

'*Spy* on people?'

She winced inwardly at his quick fury. Snippet, disturbed, rose, circled in a tail-chasing movement and settled down again.

'There is no need whatsoever,' he declared, 'for me to tell you, nor for me to defend myself to you, but I use the binoculars for a number of reasons. One, to keep an eye on this place when I'm over there——' indicating his grandmother's residence '—and two, when I'm living here, to make sure that all's well over there. You get the picture?'

Terri looked down, looked up. 'I get it.'

'Good.' But his anger still simmered.

Hopefully, Terri glanced through the window, only to have her hopes dashed yet again at the sight of the bending trees and the billowing black clouds massed over the mountains.

From across the room came the ring of the telephone, startling Terri to her depths.

Brendan strolled across and answered, 'Yes, Harvey. We're OK.' He sounded long-suffering. 'Reassure my grandmother, will you? Yes, the dog's fine.' He listened, making a face. 'Is that so? Well, if we're marooned here into the wee small hours, at least we've got a roof over our heads. Cheers.' He rang off.

'The forecast?' Terri ventured. 'It's bad?'

'No let-up this side of midnight, nor any foreseen yet beyond that.' He came to stand beside her. 'Satisfied that we're under surveillance, even if it is at the end of a phone line? You're safe, Miss Butler, from my evil intentions. Not that I had any——' his eyes swept over her '—much. So far,' he said with a tight exhalation of breath, 'so good.'

He glanced down at her and she nodded, her heart hitting a high note.

This man had more than his share of good looks, she reflected, aware that not only had her heart gone slightly crazy, but so, more worryingly, had her feminine responses. She knew from his grandmother that he had no wife. He'd come near to acquiring one, Mrs Stewart had told her, but the young woman in question had waited until the eve of the wedding to tell him she had decided to resume her relationship with her former lover.

He had been so furious, his grandmother had commented, his hurt pride and disillusionment upsetting him probably more than a broken heart, that he had resolved never again to make a commitment to any woman.

Terri could not suppress an inward sigh. As her sister would have said, he was a hunk of a man. No right-thinking girl would just want an affair with him; she'd want him for life. The photograph on his grandmother's piano by no means did him justice. It portrayed a good-looking male—which, she was unnervingly aware, he certainly was—but what it had left out, because the person behind the camera had possessed a mechanical instead of a probing artistic eye, was the deep intelligence in that gaze, the 'I know where I'm going and heaven help anyone who gets in my way' look it held.

'Well,' he commented drily, 'what's my score out of ten?'

Terri coloured, annoyed with herself for having given away even a hint of her curiosity about him. If only, she thought, moving away, it had been mere curiosity. It was just as well that he hadn't been able to guess at the sensations he seemed able to arouse in her merely by being in the same room.

'I'd need a degree in mathematics,' she answered with a smile, 'to do that kind of calculation.'

'Which you don't have?'

'No,' she answered truthfully, omitting to tell him, since she did not think he'd be interested, that on leaving school she had passed her mathematics exam with flying colours, but she had not taken the subject to degree standard.

'So, since you're in possession of the facts of *my* educational background, tell me, what is yours?'

She lifted her shoulders and tucked her borrowed shirt into the waistband of her borrowed trousers. 'I have a very short *curriculum vitae*. School, college to take a secretarial course, plus general subjects. Sufficient to enable me to find a reasonable job in miscellaneous offices.'

He regarded her thoughtfully. 'Short though my acquaintance is with you, I'd say that, intellectually speaking, you're wasted on my grandmother. An unstretched mind.'

'What, *mine*?'

'Yours.'

'How can you tell?' She was honestly interested in his answer.

She didn't get one. Instead, he asked, 'What do you plan to do when you leave here, as eventually you will?'

'I like it here,' she pointed out.

He lifted his broad shoulders. 'Boredom will inevitably set in. Once the novelty of living among all this natural beauty has worn off, you'll begin to feel restless.' After a pause, he asked, 'Does—shall we say...a permanent relationship figure in your life's schedule?'

Not marriage, she noted, remembering again his grandmother's comments.

Her eyes held his. 'One day I'll find the right man. But I'd want a commitment from him.' She heard the strange challenge in her own voice.

He smiled, but to Terri his whole demeanour seemed to convey the message, Don't look at me. 'Blunt, too.' He felt his nose. 'Well, well. It's still intact. Translated into action, your outspokenness could cause serious injury.'

Terri could not help smiling.

'Since you've asked me, I can ask you. What are your plans on that subject?' she queried, aware that she was treading on mined territory, but feeling that, since he had had no inhibitions about questioning her on the subject, she could ask the same of him.

Their eyes met, hers strangely seeking, his giving nothing away.

At last he answered, 'Regarding wedded bliss?' His eyes flickered over her and his scrutiny this time had nothing to do with her mental ability and everything to do with masculine assessment. 'There's still plenty of room in my address book for another to be added. But no offers on the commitment angle. Bliss without the wedded ... yes, every time.'

Her quick colour was due to anger, not embarrassment.

'You think that every woman you meet wants to fall at your feet? I, Mr Stewart, am not one of them.'

He seemed unmoved by her outburst. Stalemate, she thought. Whose move now?

The dog's, it seemed. He rose, yawning widely into the prickling silence. Licking his lips hugely, he wandered across to where Terri had chosen to sit, on a footstool near the stone-flagged hearth. Brendan leaned forward, hand extended. The dog responded, going to him, seeming to like the stroking hand.

If I were in Snippet's place, I'd like it, too. The thought flashed in and out of Terri's thoughts, shocking her.

'Hungry, hound?' Brendan asked, totally unaware, Terri reflected thankfully, of the sudden turmoil in her mind. 'No canine food in the place.' His glance met Terri's. 'How easygoing is he where food's concerned?'

'From what Harvey says, he just takes what comes his way.'

'Good.' He rose, standing easily, hands in pockets, looking down at her. 'Your own tastes? How fastidious are you where your—er—appetite's concerned?'

Was it, she wondered, a double-edged question? She replied to it in a double-edged way. '*Very*. Except that, in the digestive sense, I usually accept whatever's put in front of me.' Her face tilted upwards, her smile asking him, Shall we agree on a draw?

His answering smile was brief, promising fresh moves up his sleeve which would give 'checkmate' and victory to him.

Snippet mopped up some small pieces of canned meat from an old enamel plate that Brendan had placed on the floor, drinking thirstily the water that Brendan offered him.

Terri kept her word and demolished the canned fish that she had helped Brendan arrange on a bed of the fresh salad ingredients he had brought from town that day. They drank tea in front of the stove, basking in its warmth. Conversation was spasmodic but reasonably friendly. She guessed that, like herself, her host was no good with small talk.

She found herself regretting the fact. Only by talking, she felt, would she get to know this grandson of her employer. And she found herself *wanting* to get to know him. It was that wanting that worried her unduly.

CHAPTER THREE

THE washing of the dishes behind them, Terri stared out at the darkening landscape. 'What chance——?' she began tautly, but he cut across the question.

'None. Not in this storm.'

A storm, Terri was forced to admit, was what it had undoubtedly become. Distant pine trees bent and twisted as the gale lashed them, wild waves invaded the inlet. The Atlantic Ocean had beaten its way even into that safe haven.

The windows, which rattled alarmingly, seemed to have absorbed some of the blackness outside. With the help of the oil lamp which Brendan had lit, she saw reflected in them his tall figure, arms folded, standing behind her. He seemed to be watching her intently.

His scrutiny disturbed her. To ease the strange tension, she appealed to his overpowering reflection. 'Couldn't I leave the boat on this side and walk back along the road you came by this afternoon?'

An irritable intake of breath was released, then, 'OK.' He had responded too briskly for her to believe that he had accepted her suggestion. 'Come with me,' he said, in a 'you asked for it' tone.

He took her arm but she hung back. 'I must get a jacket.'

He gave her no chance, propelling her to the door, flinging it wide and urging her outside. She was robbed of breath, her hair streaming across her face, the chill of the gale striking cruelly through the thin layers of clothing that she wore.

'Had enough?'

She nodded vigorously, glad of the warmth he allowed her to retreat back into.

Pushing back the hair from her eyes, she asked, sounding as helpless as she felt, 'What now?'

'You'll spend the night here. You and the hound. You'll stay until morning. OK?' His hand lifted to silence her as she made to protest.

Not OK, she had been about to say, but admitted out loud that she supposed she had no choice.

'Now we've got that straight——' He consulted his watch. 'Too soon for bed.' He folded his arms.

Her heart jolted as she remembered that the cottage possessed only one.

'We could read.' He indicated the bookshelves. 'Or listen to music.' He paused, unfolded his arms and pushed his hands into his belt. 'Get to know each other better.'

Her head shot up. 'I told you, no.'

Broad shoulders rose and fell. 'So...' He went to his bag and extracted a radio-cum-tape-recorder, detaching the stereo speakers and placing them on the table. 'Do you like classical music? Just as well, because that's all there is on these tapes.'

He switched it on, having rearranged two low chairs. Sinking into one, he indicated to Terri that she should do the same. Bemused, she did so, immediately ensnared by the beautiful sounds that filled her head.

Brendan leaned back, stretching out his long legs, closing his eyes and spreading his expressive hands on the arms of the chair. At first, Terri was too tense to relax so completely, but as the music reached her deepest being she followed his example and gave herself up to the swelling, emotional harmonies.

As the music died away, she opened her eyes to find him watching her again. In his look there was assessment and—was she imagining it?—the minutest touch of suspicion. But beneath all that there was some-

thing else that had her heartbeats jumping and her voice
wanting to shout, No!

Perhaps, after all, there hadn't been a question, just
a reflective kind of wondering…as to how long it would
take him to change her mind? Or even what sort of in-
centive he would need to offer, to alter her negative into
a positive response?

The tape came to an end and he got up to switch it
off. 'More?' he queried, standing in front of her.

So, she thought with a sense of relief, and something
else that was too complicated to work out, I was wrong
in my assumption that he was that sort of guy.

'Thanks, but no,' she answered, yawning. 'If it isn't
too early to turn you out of your living-room——'

'I'll sleep in here. You're having the bed.'

'But it's yours. Thanks, but——'

'Tonight, Miss Butler, it's yours.'

'Please, my name's Terri.'

'And mine is Brendan. As if,' with a faint twist of the
mouth, 'you didn't know. I'm sorry.' He led the way
upstairs, expecting her to follow. 'I haven't had time to
change the bedclothes. They've only been used once, but
in there——' he indicated a cupboard with a slightly
crooked door '—is a pile of sheets and whatever.'

'You mean,' she remarked over her shoulder, drawing
the curtains over the dark windows, 'you're remembering what I said about being fastidious?' She shook
her head. 'I'm so tired I think I could even sleep on the
stones out there. But I wish you——'

His hand moved, covering her mouth. At the sudden
familiarity of his touch, her pulses leapt, the air momentarily trapped in her lungs. He stared at her with an
intensity that brought the colour to her cheeks. Did he
think she was giving him the signals he had earlier been
looking for?

All he said was, 'I'll be OK in my sleeping-bag on the hearthrug. Make yourself at home. The bathroom's yours. There are clean towels in the linen store.'

'Thanks for being so thoughtful.'

He nodded and left. Some time later, as she tiptoed from the bathroom, Terri smiled as she heard his voice downstairs telling Snippet to have the courtesy to shake the rain from his coat before coming back into a civilised man's living-room.

The bed was large and she felt somewhat lost in it, stretching her legs into the empty spaces, then pulling them back as though they had trespassed. All the time, her nostrils were assailed by the scent of the man whose clothes a few hours before she had so unthinkingly borrowed.

Now that she knew the human being to whom it belonged, the aroma troubled something inside her. She found herself curling up, face burrowing into the pillow, inhaling as if that 'something' was itching to get more and more of it into her system. And the thought frightened her.

Lying there, she coaxed sleep to take over, but it proved so maddeningly elusive that she gave in to her over-active mind and allowed it free rein in its efforts to think out a plot for that story she intended to write.

There would be a girl—name of Theresa? Why shouldn't it be her own?—and a man. His name could be—no, not Brendan! But Brandon; surely that would fit into the story... What story? Her tired brain started to go round in circles.

The gale—it must surely be force ten?—curled and roared around the house, howling through every gap and crack in the cottage's defences. Even the windows rattled as if they were frightened by the gale's ferocity. There was no light at all and Terri began to wish that there were a flashlight within reach which she could use to reassure herself that the dark corners of the room were

not peopled by—heaven knew what. She began to wish
that her imagination were not so active that it made her
teeth start to chatter.

Her hand stretched out to the flat top of the small
chest that stood beside the bed, but no light met her
groping hand. At that moment there came a snorting
beneath the bedroom door. As the small yelp of frustration hit her ears, her hand came up against an object
that fell with a crash which, in the pitch-darkness, and
tense as she was, tore a scream from her throat.

Seconds later there came the sound of pattering paws
and of feet taking the stairs swiftly. The door burst open
and the dark corners of the room which seemed to have
been advancing closer by the minute receded fast. The
trembling body of a small dog flung itself on to the bed,
whining and sniffing and generally conveying the idea
that the occupant of that bed had abandoned her canine
companion totally uncaringly to its fate.

'Snippet, oh, Snippet!' Terri exclaimed, sitting up and
hugging him to her. 'Am I pleased to see you!'

She did her best to dodge his licking tongue at one
end and his madly waving tail at the other. He quietened
at last and Terri's eyes lifted to rest on the male figure
that now stood dauntingly, arms folded, a few steps from
the entrance. His dominating outline was illuminated by
the glow of the flashlight he held.

'It's—it's all right for you,' Terri told that somewhat
arrogant figure. 'You—you're probably used to the tor-
nadoes and typhoons and things they get in this part of
the country. All I wanted was a light. I hoped I'd find
one on this bedside table, but all that happened was a
great crash, and——'

'I heard.' The tall figure moved round the room to
inspect the damage. There had been no sound of
breaking glass, Terri remembered thankfully.

'I'll pay for whatever I've broken,' she told him,
peering down.

'It'll cost you all your savings,' came the satiric answer as Brendan rose, holding a battery-powered bedside lamp. 'It's intact. It's made entirely of plastic. Aren't you lucky?'

He re-positioned the lamp, switching it on. He stood towering over her, hands on hips which were only partially covered, Terri now noticed with a shock, by briefs which truly lived up to their name, and over which hung an unbuttoned shirt.

Her gaze swung quickly from the potent manliness which, even in the semi-darkness, the briefs did little to hide, climbing upwards over the lean-cut waist to a chest which boasted a dark mat of hair. Her eyes shifted upwards again to shoulders, the breadth of which were not concealed by the shirt. His expression, however, she could not see.

'No dogs allowed on the bed. Nor in the bedroom.'

He followed the pronouncement with immediate action, scooping a protesting dog from Terri's arms and depositing him firmly on the other side of the door.

Deprived of the dog's companionship, Terri's ears picked up the sounds of the storm. They tuned in to the moaning wind, and she remembered the blackness that had prevailed before the crash of the lamp and Snippet's eruption into the room.

'Please let Snippet stay,' she whispered, eyes large with tiredness. 'He'd be a comfort. He'd reassure me that I wasn't the only living creature in the place, and that——'

'You want reassurance? You want comfort? OK, move over. It's my side of the bed you're occupying.'

Share the bed with this fantastic specimen of manhood? she asked herself. The idea horrified, and— she could not deny it—excited her so much, she was shocked to the core.

'No! No, thank you. I'm—I'll be f-fine. You just— just stop worrying about me. Go back to your——'

'Sleeping-bag? When I'm constantly being nudged off the hearthrug by a small dog with big ideas about his own personal space? And when there's all this bed going spare? Oh, no, not on your sweet——' his eyes in the semi-darkness took on an unmistakably unchaste expression '—very sweet life.'

Outside the closed door, Snippet sniffed at its base, gave a yelp of frustration and pattered down to return to his place on the hearthrug.

'If you do...' why, Terri wondered, had her throat become so dry? '...I'll...' Useless to threaten when it was *his* bed, and *his* cottage. 'You must——' what must he do? '—keep to your side of the bed.'

'OK.'

His tone was so amenable, she grew suspicious. And with reason, she soon discovered.

As he stooped to peel back the bedcover, she gasped. The action revealed that the large T-shirt she had borrowed from him had worked high enough to expose her thighs, not to mention the rest of her legs. With frantic movements, she tugged at the hem, but his fingers round her wrist prevented her from succeeding in covering herself.

'Let a man admire the scenery. After all, you have to agree that ever since you arrived on my doorstep I've been unstinting in the hospitality I've offered you. Yes?'

His smile taunted, but she could only echo his 'yes', not as a question, but as an affirmative.

Giving her no chance to persist with her modest actions, he slid his arms beneath her armpits and her knees, lifting her bodily and tossing her protesting figure across the bed.

'*My* side, I believe you said?' He fell on to the bed, the mattress sagging under his weight.

Her head turned on the pillow and her eyes grew large as they rested on the virile male body beside her. Never before had she...

'New experience?'

He must have picked up her thoughts. Should she tell him? 'Maybe it is, maybe it isn't.'

An eyebrow flicked high, those eyes roamed again.

'I'm tired,' she offered hopefully into the semi-darkness, at which he laughed aloud.

'OK, OK. I can take a hint.' Then, to her relief, but also perversely, to her disappointment, he turned on to his side away from her, switched off the light, then pulled the cover over his shoulder.

'Goodnight,' he said.

She answered in a whisper and, following his example, turned from him.

In spite of her very best efforts, sleep stayed obstinately out of her reach. The deep breathing of the man beside her was louder than the howl of the gale, and also, she discovered to her cost, infinitely more disturbing. She had longed for reassurance and comfort. She had, she discovered, exchanged the ferocity of the elements for the far greater wildness of the beating of her heart.

In the dim light, she could, if she swivelled her head, see the slope of his shoulder, the tiny hairs that covered the tops of his arms like down. She wanted to rub her cheek against them, run her finger down the sweep of the resolute jaw. Ordering her feminine reflexes to quieten down and leave her alone, she tried again to let her limbs and muscles slacken, but without success.

Her body turned itself, first to the left, then to the right. She sought for tranquillity, but with this man beside her she knew she would never find it, given a thousand years.

She turned again, her back to him. The mattress sank and rose as he turned, too, and a deep sigh stroked her ear. When two arms came out, one moving across her, the other pushing under her shoulders, she found herself accepting them, without the slightest desire to push them away.

'Will you relax, for heaven's sake?' came the sharp, if husky order. And she did, deeply and completely, allowing sleep to claim her at last.

Daylight came early, bringing with it the realisation that not only was she not in her own room in the house of Mrs Christiana Stewart, but she was in a room she had never before seen in daylight. Moreover, and much more disturbing, she was sharing a bed with a strange man!

Except that, when she turned her startled gaze towards that man, she realised that he was by no means a stranger, but that she had spent some hours the previous day in his company.

'Hi.'

As a word, it was simple and straightforward. As a greeting, acceptable and friendly. It was the look in the eyes of the speaker that had her limbs stiffening in apprehension and—surely not—anticipation? Her instinct to escape fought alarmingly with her even greater instinct to stay.

It was as if it were not herself but another person who watched the man beside her lift himself on to his elbow and gaze down at her, a primitive kind of half-smile curving his expressive mouth.

It was, she concluded, definitely another person who watched that mouth slowly descend, making no effort to evade its eventual touchdown on her own; who not only tolerated the feel of that mouth on hers but who positively enjoyed the sensations it was arousing.

When at the same time an arm slid under her shoulders and a hand found its way beneath the T-shirt to cover a burgeoning breast, her throat rasped on a gasp of protest at the same time as her body started to yield to the unrelenting persuasion of that determined hand and two searching, persistent lips.

When the telephone extension shrieked itself into a frenzy in a corner of the room, that mouth dragged itself from hers with a smothered curse. Bare muscular legs thrust from under the cover and at speed took their owner across to seize the instrument as if it had done him an injury.

'Yes?' he barked as he carried the phone across and sat, his back to Terri, on the bed. 'Grandmother? Do you know what time it is? Yes, six o'clock in the *morning*. Interrupted my beauty sleep? Or,' with a drawl, 'my *beauty's* sleep?' with a quick, raking glance at the dishevelled figure beside him. 'Yes to both.'

He swivelled sideways and listened, his expression long-suffering.

'No,' he responded at last, 'I have not violated the lady.' His swift glance at Terri flashed a mocking 'yet'. 'Even though,' he went on, 'we're sharing a bed. *The* bed. Yes,' wearily now, 'I tried the hearthrug. Have *you* ever tried sleeping on a hearthrug? No, I thought not.' He listened again, a closed expression shutting out his thoughts. Another sigh, then, 'Grandmother, you have my word on that score. Only when the woman is irresistible and the invitation's blatant do I...' With a rueful expression, he held the receiver a short distance from his ear, waited a few moments, then continued, 'Sorry I offend your sensibilities, Grandmother. I get the drift. Hands off the person in question it will be.'

Seemingly unsatisfied with the reassurance, the insistent caller apparently persisted.

'Have no fear, Grandmother. As soon as this unmentionable weather allows, I'll return the lady in question safe and entirely sound to your protective keeping.'

Putting the telephone aside, he swung his legs back on to the bed. Terri, worried about his next move, but more anxious about her own responses to that move, simultaneously swung her own legs to the floor, only to find her arm grabbed and her tensing self pulled back beside him.

'No!' she exclaimed breathily, using all her energy to withstand the attraction of his solid torso, his hair-sprinkled thighs, his toughly muscled legs. 'Don't touch me. You're not getting any "blatant invitations" from me.'

His glance slid over her face. 'You didn't like my choice of words?' His smile was slow and lazy. 'You object to the implication that I don't find you irresistible?'

She shook free of his hold and scrambled from the bed. 'I *object* to your colossal arrogance, your male chauvinism. In fact, I refuse to share this bed with you any longer.'

She followed his eyes and blushed to find that the shirt he had lent her had again ridden high over her thighs. As she tugged it down, she threw him a furious look, knowing full well that what he had not been able to see he had used his imagination to conjure up.

'Lady,' came from him softly, his gaze following her as she made for the door, 'if you think that, before the phone rang, I was behaving towards you in an *ungentle-manly* fashion, then you must know very little indeed about the male of the species.'

The fact that he was right about her inexperience only served to heighten her pique. She slammed the door behind her and ran down the stairs, making for the hearthrug, sliding into Brendan Stewart's sleeping-bag and curling up beside the still-somnolent dog.

Waking, she stirred, needing to orientate herself all over again. Not only no familiar, well-furnished bedroom in a substantially built residence, but no bed either, just a soft kind of wrapping around her.

Her memory came to life and one by one the course of events since she left Mrs Christiana Stewart's house the day before fell into place. Wriggling free of the sleeping-bag, she folded it and stowed it in a corner. Tiptoeing up the stairs, she sighed with relief on discovering that the bedroom door was half-open and the room itself empty.

She pulled on a robe which she found hanging on the back of the door, gathered the clothes, now dried, which she had worn the day before, and made for the bathroom. Fifteen minutes later she emerged, bathed, dressed and greatly refreshed.

Using her ears as a means of judging in which room the owner of the property was hiding, she descended the stairs into the small hallway. A glance into the living-room told her that he was not there. Nor, she noted with something of a shock, was Snippet, which could only mean that Brendan had taken him for a walk.

To make quite sure, she called, raising her voice, 'Brendan? Mr Stewart? Are you there?' No reply.

Which meant, also, that she was, for the first time, alone in the place. The impact of the brighter weather on her brain had brought her imagination to life.

Now's your chance, it was urging her, to look around, search for ideas for that story you've been commissioned to write—yes, *commissioned*, she thought with a burst of pleasure, even though it was only by her sister.

She turned from the kitchen entrance to find a closed door to one side of the hall. A closed door... Did that room that Brendan had mentioned lurk behind it? The room that had seemed so important, so private to him? Yet he had said that it was not locked.

A moment of concentrated listening followed by a hurried glance around assured her that she was still alone. A turn of the handle proved that his statement had been correct.

Through its uncurtained window shone the bright morning sun. Her blood ran faster. She had penetrated his hideaway! Her eyes darted round, her imagination filling empty spaces—with what? Electronic equipment?

she pondered. Secret files? There was no computer in sight—it wouldn't, she concluded, work properly via a generator.

The files were there, stacks of them, plus a couple of filing cabinets and folders and weighty volumes on shelves around the walls. She read the books' titles, withdrawing one or two and leafing through them, but even with her knowledge of scientifically based subjects, sufficient though it had been to get her through her college exams with reasonably good marks, she couldn't comprehend their contents.

A portable typewriter stood on a desk, the top of which was covered with paper, handwritten and printed, with figures and graphs and something which resembled mathematical formulae.

Her imagination went into overdrive. So what was his position in life, this man who had offered her hospitality, albeit none too willingly, in her hour of need, and with whom she had actually shared a bed? More important, *who was he*? Her employer's grandson, yes, she knew that, something in the academic world, but what else?

She drew her notebook and pencil from her jeans pocket. 'When ideas are found,' her journalist sister had once told her, 'make a note of them. Never rely on your memory.' So she scribbled a few lines, a kind of word picture, she told herself, of her host's hideaway, secret sanctuary...wouldn't that, she mused, make a good title?

At the sound of scampering paws, she crammed the paper and pencil back into her pocket, at the same time backing out and, noiselessly, she hoped, closing the door. A growling, playful bark had her swinging round and stooping to retrieve the stick from Snippet's mouth.

'You silly animal,' she reprimanded him, laughing, 'you were meant to deliver this at the feet of the man who threw it for you—— Oh, hi.' She straightened to find Brendan, expression quizzical, looking down at her.

Agitated, although she didn't know why, she smiled uncertainly up at him. 'Snippet gave this to me instead of you.'

Holding it out, she watched his hand come out to take it from her. That reserve of his was back, in his eyes, his body movements, his demeanour. Taking the stick, he threw it into the bucket which held the logs for the stove, which was no longer alight.

It seemed to be necessary to fill the prickly silence, so she offered, 'You took Snippet for a walk.'

'A brilliant deduction.' Even his tone had changed, edged now with cynicism. 'Have you breakfasted? No? Then we'll breakfast together, shall we?' His mouth tilted with a taunting kind of amusement. 'Like any other civilised couple who've shared a bed.'

'Thanks for the invitation, but I have to get back.' She added with a touch of asperity that surprised even herself, 'Unlike you, I'm not a guest at your grandmother's house, I'm her employee.'

'Even a perfect secretary, which I'm sure you are,' he said with a mocking glint in his eye, 'must eat. And correction. Nor am *I* a guest. Not only do I belong here, but my reason for coming at this precise moment in time is completely above board.'

Implying, Terri told herself with a frown, that mine isn't? Well, she had no time to work out that particular puzzle. The pad of letters which her employer had dictated before she, Terri, had been granted the afternoon off—and what an afternoon it had been, not to mention evening, night and now morning!—nagged at her mind.

'Thank you for your hospitality. And for saving me from the elements. Without your appearance on the scene,' she smiled, 'I would probably have suffered from a severe case of hypothermia.'

She found his frown somewhat intimidating. 'Don't joke about such a serious matter. That affliction is not a matter of *life* and death. Hypothermia's a matter of *death*. It can be a killer.'

'I'm—I'm sorry,' she returned with sincerity. 'In that case, I should be thanking you for saving my life.'

The look he gave her was intense and assessing, and just a little unnerving, but his only response was to shrug.

He watched as she lifted her jacket—wrong, she thought, Brendan Stewart's jacket—from the clothes-airer in front of the fire and started to pull it on.

'Where do you think you're going?'

She stopped, one arm in one sleeve. 'Back to the house. Why?'

'By what means of transport?'

'The way I arrived—by boat.'

'You're intending to row yourself back across the inlet?'

'Yes. And the dog, of course.'

'Have you looked outside?'

'It's a warm and sunny morning. Why?'

'Sunny it may be, but warm it's not. What's more, it's hellish windy.'

He was right. It was even back to rattling the windows, having risen in the last twenty minutes or so.

'You think,' he went on, his brows rising mockingly, 'you really think you've got sufficient strength in your secretarial arms to get yourself—and the hound, *of course*,' with sarcasm, 'to pull the oars against the current, not to mention that gale out there?'

'I——' She frowned, uncertain now. 'The outboard motor——?'

'Not working. I tried it.' He eyed her up and down as she buttoned the jacket. 'You're determined, are you, to end your life in some way, any way that's handy? Yesterday, you tried the method of dying of exposure. Today, you're aiming to drown yourself?'

At last he had aroused her ire. 'Don't be silly. Yesterday I didn't do it deliberately. I told you, I haven't been in this area long enough to forecast the changes in the weather. Anyway, I love life. I'm enjoying every minute of it.'

'OK. I'm glad we've got that straight. So go on enjoying it. *I* shall row you across. I made a promise to my grandmother to return you safe and sound, so return you I will.'

'OK,' she said with a sigh. 'But,' she added with a winning curve of her lips, '*before* breakfast, please?'

'With a smile like that,' he commented, motioning her outside and whistling to the dog, 'you could get away with murder... almost.'

Tossed by the waves, the small craft battled across the inlet. Terri would not admit, even to herself, that she was afraid. Who could be, she asked herself, with a man like Brendan Stewart at the helm, with his strength to ward off calamities, with his mental prowess to guide you through life's tangled pathways?

Stop, she told her runaway imagination, inventing purple passages—her sister had told her about those, too—while in dire danger of being swept away by wind and waves. And stop building up this man, this *ordinary* man, into something larger than life. But he wasn't ordinary, was he? He was special, very special indeed ...

CHAPTER FOUR

TERRI came back to reality when a particularly large wave tossed them sideways. Brendan righted the boat with consummate ease, glancing her way.

'You OK?' he asked. At her nod, he returned to his battle with the waves.

He had donned a life-jacket, insisting that Terri should do the same. Holding the dog close, she watched, fascinated, as the muscular arms pulled them across to the other shore. The journey, which had seemed so short in the calm conditions of the day before, now seemed never-ending.

They arrived at last, and Snippet leapt from her hold, pawing himself upwards on to firm ground. Standing, Brendan steadied the boat and Terri scrambled to her feet. The boat rocked and, with a cry, she lost her balance, her arms groping for support and finding it in the strong arms that had pulled them so safely across.

For a long, heart-racing moment, those arms held her upright, then, without warning, lifted her bodily. Grey eyes held hers, the usually rather austere mouth curved ever so faintly, and a shiver took hold which, Terri knew, had no origin in the cooling effect of the wind.

They were steely, those grey eyes, and perceptive, holding a resolution that engendered both reassurance and a curious kind of fear.

'I'm—I'm quite capable of getting myself on to dry land, thank you,' she managed, feeling strangely unnerved by all that her intuition was telling her... or was it, she wondered, her imagination?

Ignoring her statement, he took a measured stride over the now shallow water on to firm ground. His smile taunted her as he held her for a few more tantalising moments, then lowered her to her feet.

Snippet, having exhausted all the aromatic possibilities of the nearby terrain, sat on his haunches and uttered a series of short, reprimanding barks. Terri found herself laughing with Brendan. Shared laughter with this man, she thought, is a wonderful experience...

'Stop that racket, hound,' growled Brendan and, to Terri's astonishment, Snippet obeyed.

Brendan came up behind her and even through the layers she wore she felt the impact of him. When his hand came to rest on her arm, she jumped, her head jerking round.

'What do you——?'

'Want? The life-jacket, that's all. What else would I *want*, hmm?'

Facing forward so that he would not see the quick colour in her cheeks, she loosened the front ties and allowed him to free her from the inflated garment. Its air rushed out and he placed it, folded, on top of his own, holding them both under his arm.

'Come on, Snippet, race me,' Terri called. The dog joined in the game and beat her to the house, climbing the bank of coarse grasses to the rocky ground on which the house stood.

They arrived breathless, Snippet's tail working madly, Terri's gaze swinging round to discover that Brendan was striding to join them. The door came open and Harvey welcomed them back with his customary slightly dour expression.

Terri smiled and nodded. As she rubbed her shoes on the mat, Snippet dashed past her, making for the kitchen. Behind her on the top step, Brendan greeted Harvey, who had, for his employer's grandson, turned on a genuine smile of welcome.

Having donned house shoes, Terri made for the sweeping staircase. Halting three steps up, she called to Harvey, 'Mrs Stewart—she's decent, isn't she?'

'Oh, aye, she's decent enough. You know by now that she dresses for bed as if she's going out for a stroll.'

Terri laughed. For some reason, life felt better than ever. Her glance, of its own accord, sought and bounced off the face of her employer's grandson. No need to search for the reason; it stood down there, hands in pockets, life-jackets put aside, feet firmly planted on the doormat. I belong here, his demeanour told her, which you don't.

Mrs Stewart sat straight-backed against a pile of pillows, looking over the items on her breakfast tray. She glanced up, unsurprised, her keen eyes missing nothing of Terri's bright exuberance.

'My grandson,' she remarked as Terri moved to stand beside her bed. 'Has he behaved himself? Yes,' before Terri could reply, 'I can see for myself that he heeded my warning. For the duration of your employment with me, I have assumed the role of *in loco parentis*. I will have no man, related to me or not, helping himself to your attractions and your young womanhood outside the marital status.'

She watched the colour sweep across Terri's face, then resumed the minute contemplation of the contents of her breakfast tray.

'Not—not even with my consent?' Terri, slightly to her own dismay, heard herself ask.

Grey eyes, sharp as her grandson's, sought Terri's. They revealed shock tempered with resignation.

'Young women today.' Mrs Stewart shook her head. 'They are so foolish. They have lost the art of being just that little bit beyond a man's reach. They are no longer ever so slightly mysterious, nor do they even attempt to keep a man guessing. On the contrary, they throw themselves at the male of the species. Thus they make the wrong choice, and so,' with a sigh, 'the marriage doesn't last.'

'Grandmother.' Brendan stood in the doorway, every inch the male of the species to whom the speaker had referred.

He had changed from boots to shoes, from slightly tattered pullover to a darker, more presentable one. He had replaced his faded jeans with well-fitting navy denims, into whose pockets he now slid his hands.

There was no mistaking the pleasure in the white-haired lady's face as it lifted in greeting.

'Brendan.' Her arms came out and her grandson moved into them, bending down and accepting the warm kiss on his cheek, returning it gently.

Straightening, his lazy eyes came to rest on his grandmother's employee. 'Watch your breakfast tray, Grandmother,' was his mocking comment. 'Your companion, secretary, lady driver, whatever, has designs on Harvey's culinary efforts.'

'You're hungry, dear?' Mrs Stewart inspected Terri's features. 'Didn't Brendan offer you any food before bringing you across?'

'I did,' Brendan took up the question, 'but the lady was in such a hurry to get back to you, she not only refused my offerings, she insisted that I should postpone *my* meal and bring her back first.'

With a finger that showed not the slightest tremor, Mrs Stewart pointed to the toast pushed into the stainless-steel rack. 'Help yourself, my dear.'

Terri began to do her employer's bidding. But Brendan moved quickly, coming round the bed and seizing her hand.

Shaken, Terri looked down at the well-tended, rounded nails, liking the feel of the fingers wrapped around her wrist. Suppressing at once her feelings on that particular subject, she protested, 'But I'm hungry——'

A light tap on the door had her watching wide-eyed as Harvey entered, carefully carrying an overflowing tray to a trolley which he proceeded to wheel across the room. The aroma of coffee filled the air, the sight of tomatoes and scrambled eggs piled high on succulent toast almost driving Terri's taste-buds crazy.

'Ten out of ten for consideration and thoughtfulness, Miss Butler?' Brendan queried sarcastically.

'Or was it thoughtfulness on Harvey's part?' Mrs Stewart prompted with a smile. 'Yes, Harvey?'

'Och no, madam. Mr Brendan requested that I should provide food for two ravenous people. I assumed those to be——' His nod indicated Terri and the man who still had her hand in his keeping.

'That's very kind of you, Harvey,' Terri remarked just before he closed the door behind him. Without much success she endeavoured to free her hand. 'And,' she added with a glance at Brendan, 'thanks for your kindly act. Now, will you please——?'

'Release you to satisfy your appetite? Give me one good reason why I should. You failed to satisfy *my*——'

'Please!' She cast a horrified glance in her employer's direction.

'I'm glad to hear it,' came blandly from that lady as she forked a piece of lean bacon into her mouth. 'Which is as it should be. Now, will you stop playing the fool, Brendan, and——? That's right, dear,' she said as her grandson, with undisguised reluctance, did her bidding. 'Pull up a chair for Terri, and——' she patted the bed '—sit yourself down here.'

Ten minutes later, Terri leaned back in her chair with a satisfied sigh.

'Has that taken the edge off your appetite?' Brendan asked, sinking white teeth into a slice of toast spread liberally with marmalade. 'Or was the egg and tomato merely an appetiser?'

Terri eyed the small cereal packet which stood next to a jug filled with creamy milk, but managed to resist its siren call. She shook her head and patted her middle, immediately wishing that she hadn't, since Brendan's ever-vigilant gaze was immediately drawn to it.

Removing her hand, she rested it on her knee, but his eyes moved there. He was, she was convinced, mentally reducing her to the flimsily dressed state she had been in when occupying one half of his bed.

'Don't you ever,' she challenged in an undertone, unfairly, she was honest enough to admit, taking advantage of Mrs Stewart's slight deafness, 'switch off?'

Guessing her meaning, he put back his head and laughed.

'Is she putting you in your place, young man?' asked his grandmother with a faint smile, draining her coffee-cup. 'About time someone did.'

'She's telling me, Down, Fido. If I sat up and panted and begged——' his smile taunted '—would you be able to resist my request?'

Terri could not suppress an answering smile. 'Easily.' Put to the test, she was forced to acknowledge, she knew for certain that she would not.

Those grey eyes which had been so cold when she had appeared on his particular scene could, she knew now by experience, coerce and coax and—almost—seduce. How she had resisted their seduction as he had lain beside her she would never know, but resist them she had, and, as sure as summer followed spring, she would have to go on doing so.

She could, she told herself, fall headlong for this hunk of maleness, even following him to the rainbow's end if he asked. But, she vowed, fall she would not. I'll stay on my emotional feet, she promised herself, and if he were to walk away, hand stretching back for mine to slide into it, I'd use all my mental strength and turn from it, walk the other way. Wouldn't I?

* * *

Terri took Mrs Stewart shopping. The surrounding rugged mountains dwarfed the little town, their summits, even in early summer, being coated, like icing, with snow.

As her employer gossiped with the store owners and assistants, Terri stared around. She found herself delighting in the colours of the tartans on display, stretching her hand to enjoy the feel of the pure wool, which promised warmth even on the coldest of days. She stroked long-haired sheepskin rugs, squeezed woollen sweaters and liked the way they sprang back when released.

She was in the act of selecting a tartan scarf when Mrs Stewart glanced round.

'No, no, my dear,' she called across the shop, 'that's the wrong choice.' With a twinkle in her eye she said, 'It's the Stewart clan you'll have to be loyal to while you're working for me. Here——' She motioned to the assistant to select the correct tartan. 'I will pay for your purchase. No,' she said as Terri started to protest, 'I insist.'

While her employer disappeared into her favourite hairdressing salon, Terri, on her instructions, bought herself some clothes—jackets and sweaters and skirts, all warm enough, as Mrs Stewart had directed, to be able to withstand everything the Scottish weather could throw at her.

She wore the scarf as she drove Mrs Stewart back to the house, although the warmer temperature as the sun rose higher did not really merit it. Escorting her employer up the steps and into the house, she returned to put the car away. As she secured the garage doors, she heard footsteps and swung round.

'I knew it was trouble!' she exclaimed, gazing at the mocking face that was only inches from hers. 'I could sense it.'

'You could, could you?' Close as Brendan was, Terri knew that he wouldn't miss the sudden brightness in her eyes. She hoped he couldn't hear the thud of her traitorous heart.

He withdrew his hands from his pockets and slowly reached out. Backing away, she found herself trapped by the garage doors.

'What do you——?' she began, to discover only too plainly his intention.

He lifted the ends of the scarf which she had decided not to remove along with her jacket. 'Dress Stewart,' he commented with a smile. 'Meant for special occasions. And this——' he crossed the ends over her throat, at the same time pulling her closer '—is a special occasion.'

Lips cool but sensual, casual yet with intent, descended on hers.

With a split-second to go, she tried in vain to turn her head. 'No, please,' she protested, but, she thought ruefully, she might just as well have been talking to herself.

'Submit,' he growled, 'or I'll——' He tightened the scarf.

Her legs turned to the consistency of jelly. Against its better judgement, her mouth did as he had commanded, parting as he played with it, her arms lifting to his shoulders. To her dismay, they clung to them, her mouth all this time allowing his lips to take all kinds of liberties.

Meanwhile, her arms slipped around his back, while his, in response, went round her, leashing her to him. She felt the strength of his hips as they pressed against hers, the powerful thighs muscling in on hers, creating a low-down throb.

Slowly, he drew away, staring into her face, which was flushed now with excitement and pleasure, mixed with a feeling of guilt that she had submitted so readily to his approaches.

'That,' he said, imprisoning her with hands that rested on each side of her against the garage doors, 'is how you should have responded to me in the wee small hours.'

His essential Scottishness, she noted, was coming through in more ways than one: in his determination to win against the female of the species, in his overt desire to succeed despite all opposition.

'You,' she commented, trying desperately to regain her composure and also to bring the situation back to normal, 'would, I'm quite sure, look just—just great in a kilt.'

His head went back in laughter. It lingered in his eyes as he commented, 'I do possess a kilt. One day I might wear it. Then,' with an ironic glint, 'I might, with a little coaxing, give a lady the answer to that much repeated question.'

Knowing what he meant, Terri smiled but could not stop her blush from spreading. 'I thought,' she offered, 'that it was a well-kept secret what a man wore——'

'Och aye, it is.' He was, she knew, deliberately emphasising his Scottishness.

Snippet bounced up to them, sitting and looking from one to the other, tail working, tongue lolling.

'Hi,' commented an unrepentant Brendan. 'So who are you going to follow, hound?' He ran a hand along the wiry body. 'Take your choice. The lady's taking the high road, while I'm taking the low road. And,' he said with a tormenting look in Terri's direction, 'if I can be forgiven for misquoting, I'll be in *paradise* afore ye.'

Snippet at his heels, Brendan set off at a trot down to the road, whistling the song whose words he had just spoken.

That his last sentence had been full of meaning Terri was acutely aware. It had, she deduced, been his way of informing her that, kiss or no kiss, he would, without any difficulty, find fulfilment, fleeting though it might be, with a woman whose scruples were not as closely adhered to as she clung to hers. A woman who, in other words, would give him what he wanted without soul-searching, without any demand for commitment.

So what? she thought. But she knew, deep down, that she wouldn't be able easily to shrug off the curious twist of pain his words had caused.

She made for her room, where she stared out of the window, wondering where Brendan had gone. The mist had lifted from the nearby hills, which stood bold and clear against a blue sky. Last evening's gale had been tamed to a breeze. There was not even a hint of the clouds whose contents had descended so heavily that they had kept her prisoner—some gaoler she'd had, she thought—the night before.

Before taking Mrs Stewart to town, she had changed into her own clothes—a white blouse and bright blue skirt.

At the start of her employment three weeks before, Mrs Stewart had requested that, during the working day, she should dress with a kind of casual formality. At the weekends and on her days off, she had told Terri with a twinkle in her eye, she could dress how she liked, as long as she wore something!

The notes that Mrs Stewart had dictated the previous day waited in the small room that her employer called 'the office'. Some time later, Terri was tidying the typed letters into a neat pile when the sound of a car coming along the gravelled drive drew her to the window. It was low-slung, its colour, a bright scarlet, contrasting dazzlingly with the subdued hues of the surrounding majestic terrain.

In her mind its owner stood out, too, she noted with a growing dismay, the impact of his electric personality lighting up her thoughts and revealing to her just how much she was beginning to like the man, perhaps even more than like...

That owner now leaned back in the driving seat, allowing Snippet to jump across him. Then he slammed the car door behind him, pocketing the keys and striding towards the entrance door. Did her heart, Terri wondered anxiously, have to break into a Highland fling at the mere sight of him?

The sleek lines of the vehicle told her that its owner was partial to speed. Not only in the pace at which he covered the ground, she thought wryly, turning back to her desk. He was a fast worker, wasn't he, in other respects? Remember last night, she told herself, and how he . . . So don't build on that, she admonished her heart.

Attractive as he was, with his near-black hair and powerful physique, he would be assured of receiving a fast response from whichever lady on whom he chose to lavish his considerable charms.

Colour warmed her cheeks again as she remembered how readily, in his bed, she had kissed him back, not to mention outside the garage that morning. No wonder he had walked off whistling, she reflected. He'd just proved to himself yet again, hadn't he, how easy it was to break through a woman's—any woman's—defences?

In her own private living-room, Mrs Stewart was in the act of signing the final letter as Terri stood beside her when Snippet erupted into the room, followed by Brendan. He tossed a reminiscent smile in Terri's direction, his mocking eyes dwelling for a few tingling seconds on her lips.

'You have your car back, I see,' his grandmother commented, the smile that was never very far away whenever she looked at him lighting her round, still handsome face. 'Did you get a lift into the town?'

'Nope. I walked.'

'All that way? It's four miles!'

'So it is.'

'Poor little Snippet.' She fondled the dog as he sat at her feet. 'My grandson must have tired you out.'

'You think?' Brendan commented laconically. 'His tail's telling you he's ready for another four miles.'

He went down on his haunches to run a hand down the small dog's coat, his eyes swinging up to Terri as he

did so. Panicking slightly, she turned her head. Every
time he looked her way, she discovered, her blood ran
faster and she was beginning to dread that it might show.

'I should,' he commented, eyes narrowed, 'have asked
your secretary-cum-driver to take me in, shouldn't I?
After all, she owes me for having given her a bed for
the night, not to mention having rescued her from the
near-fatal consequences of her own stupidity.'

'I told you,' Terri protested. 'I'm new to the area, so
I couldn't read the weather signs——'

'Stop baiting her,' Mrs Stewart reprimanded,
'and——' she glanced from one to the other '—as for that
bed——'

Brendan rose. 'I had every intention, Grandmother,
of spending the night in a sleeping-bag in front of the
fire, but this hound muscled in on my territory.'

'I would imagine, Brendan——' Mrs Stewart's sharp
eyes moved between them again '—that you didn't put
up much of a fight against the dog.'

'I don't think he did,' Terri put in. 'Your grandson,
Mrs Stewart, decided to muscle in on *my* territory
instead.'

'*Your* territory,' he queried crushingly, 'when it was
my bed?'

Terri's hand flew to her face. 'I'm—I'm sorry. It was
kind of you to——'

'The lady wasn't,' he informed his grandmother, who
seemed puzzled by the statement, 'kind to *me.*'

'Thank goodness for that,' was her genuinely satisfied
remark as she capped the fountain-pen she still insisted
on using, dismissing ballpoint pens as 'modern contrap-
tions'. 'If she had...' she paused meaningfully '...one
of you would have had to go.'

Since she couldn't ban her grandson from the house
in which he had been bred, if not born, Terri reasoned,
Mrs Stewart could only mean her. She knew then, with
a strength of feeling that took her breath away, that she

did not want to go. She didn't want to leave the job she was beginning to enjoy way beyond her expectations.

She did not want to leave the surrounding beauty of the countryside, nor the lady who employed her, nor the grandson of that lady... This thought, and its implications, striking her like lightning, shook her to the core.

'The post,' Mrs Stewart broke into her thoughts, 'has brought me these.' She held up a sheaf of opened letters.

Terri seized on her statement with some relief. 'Oh, good,' she commented. 'I have my notepad with me.'

'There, young man,' Mrs Stewart declared. 'You see what a perfect secretary I have. Since I want to keep her, and,' with a smile, 'I most certainly do not wish to send *you* packing, you will behave yourself. Then you can both stay. You hear?'

Her grandson's smile, directed at Terri, held a touch of devilment which hers certainly did not. 'I hear. But does your *perfect* secretary?'

Terri's head shot up from readying her notebook. 'I *never* misbehave!' Immediately she realised how narrow-minded, not to mention downright prudish, that sounded. But, she reasoned, in this man's bed, hadn't she allowed him liberties which directly contradicted her words?

She was not really surprised when the dark head went back in laughter. 'No? No male of the species has ever——?'

'Brendan!' came his grandmother's scandalised tones. 'Leave us. At once!'

His head hung in mock-repentance. 'Sorry, Gran.' He was clearly role-playing, pretending to be the penitent child he no doubt once had been. It brought the smile to his grandmother's face which he had plainly been striving for.

On reaching the door, the look he turned on Terri—one which, she noted, his grandmother could not see—

was full of satire mixed with blatant sensuality. Before she could gather her wits and retaliate, he had gone.

Brendan was missing for most of the rest of the day. Terri tackled some of the letters which Mrs Stewart had dictated, then took Snippet for a walk. When she returned, she finished off the letters, put them aside for her employer's signature, and took Snippet for another walk.

Early evening, she selected a simple dress from the small selection she had brought with her. A white shirt-waister, its buttons and leather belt were a contrasting dark brown.

Wondering how to pass the time before the evening meal, she went into the corridor and wondered which room was Brendan's. One door was partly opened. Looking both ways and holding her breath, she put her head inside the room. Its aura was distinctly masculine, its furnishings plain and serviceable.

Making sure again that she was alone, Terri took a few steps inside. On the walls were pictures which were clearly left over from the childhood of a boy and which that boy had never had the time—nor the inclination?—to remove. This, she decided, had to be Brendan's room.

Leading from it was a bathroom, the musky male aroma reminding her with a pleasant—much too pleasant—shock of the clothes she had borrowed, of the pillow into which her face had burrowed the night before to keep out the whining of the wind.

Bolder now, she went to the window. The waters of the inlet were calmer. She noted with surprise that Brendan's cottage was clearly visible in the evening sunlight. No doubt he stood right here, she reflected, binoculars raised, 'keeping an eye' on his very private domain.

Leaning against the sill, she absorbed the atmosphere, breathing in once more the aroma of the man who occupied it, liking that aroma far too much for her peace of mind.

As in his hideaway cottage, there were shelves of books, much used and pushed back into place with no apparent order about them. She extracted one or two and tried to understand their contents, but found it all far too technical for her to comprehend.

As she replaced them, the telephone rang, the sound almost paralysing her. She'd do anything, she thought, to prevent someone from coming to answer it while she was trespassing... Her hand reached out and lifted the receiver, listening to the silence. It was unnerving, not to say eerie, and she found herself breathing as though she had been running.

Swallowing a gasp, she realised just how stupid she'd been even to touch the instrument. Dropping the receiver back on to its cradle, she raced on to the landing.

Reaching her own room, she calmed down at last, her brain having begun to function again. The story she had been commissioned to write was unfolding in her mind and she made some more notes in her personal notebook.

The striking of the grandfather clock in the hall informed her that at last it was time to make her way downstairs. As she closed her door behind her, she stiffened. Brendan's door was almost closed but not sufficiently to prevent her from hearing his conversation.

'It's a hell of a way by car, Drusilla,' he was saying, 'but OK, come with the others if you like. Yes, it's Bill who's hired the minibus.' Silence for a few moments. 'Bring the lot—the details of our research, the notes of the trials we've got in progress, which, fingers crossed, will give the results we're after. Use your own judgement. Yeah, I trust it as much—well, almost as much—as I trust my own.' He had plainly spoken with a smile. 'I've set things in motion at this end—the accommodation, the catering. Barry's coming, and Bill, George, Moira and so on. The whole team.'

From somewhere downstairs came a sharp bark. Clearly Snippet wanted to go outside and someone was obliging.

'Do you get a kick out of eavesdropping?'

Brendan's cold tones made her gasp and stopped her tiptoeing feet in their tracks.

He filled the doorway, hands in the pockets of well-fitting yet casual trousers, his stare as usual taking in Terri's appearance. It held no warm appreciation this time, but an aloof masculine assessment which brought the colour to her cheeks. 'Or is there some ulterior motive? And do you usually go into someone else's room without permission, or did you have a slip of the memory and thought that my room was your own?'

He'd seen her in his room? 'But I thought you were over there in your cottage.'

'I was.'

'So how...? You used your binoculars! How,' she choked, 'could you spy on me in that way?'

'*I* spy? I think you've got things the wrong way round, don't you?' He folded his arms, leaning sideways against the door-frame. 'After all, eavesdropping, as you were doing just now, could be construed, couldn't it, as another way of obtaining classified—that is, *secret* information?'

CHAPTER FIVE

MENTALLY, Terri reeled.

'Eavesdropping?' she protested, shaken and somewhat puzzled by his accusations. 'I most certainly was not. I was on my way downstairs. If I did overhear—well, your door was open. Anyway, it wasn't anything private, was it? Catering, accommodation. Friends would have to stay overnight. You're so far away here from the south of the country, that fits. And there's nothing secret about giving a party, which I assume it will be?'

His smile taunted her. 'A working party. No frills, no dancing. No kissing in the corner.'

Her puzzlement at his statement checked any response she might have made to his sarcasm. '*Working* party?'

'Outside your experience? If I called it a seminar, which is, as defined by the dictionary, a conference of specialists, would you get the gist?'

'I know what "seminar" means. It's just that this— your grandmother's residence, I mean—seems a strange place to hold a—well, a kind of technical get-together.'

'A long way from prying eyes.'

She frowned. 'You mean the Press?'

He lifted his shoulders, omitting to answer the question. 'Periodically, at my request, my grandmother opens up a part of the house that's kept serviced but closed.'

'Is that where the door I've noticed at the end of this corridor leads? It's kept locked.'

His smile was a little on the tight side. 'You've tried it? True to form, of course.'

Locked door? A memory returned, too vague to pinpoint, of those words having been used in some other context.

Terri frowned. 'What form? When before now have I tried to open locked doors? We only met a couple of days ago.'

His expression remained blank. She turned away, turned back.

'What did you mean just now by asking if I had an ulterior motive? And why,' she added, 'are you so suspicious where I'm concerned?'

The ringing of chimes had them both moving towards the stairs. The residents of Mrs Christiana Stewart's house ignored the musical, if imperious summons to dinner at their peril.

'I wish you had given me more notice, young man.' Across the table Mrs Stewart addressed her grandson with a frown. 'A phone call on arrival in the town before taking your car for servicing is not sufficient, as you must know by now.'

Which, Terri thought, finishing her after-dinner coffee, explained why Mrs Stewart had still been fretting, just before she, Terri, had set off on her rowing expedition across the inlet, about the long time that had elapsed since seeing her grandson.

'You know very well,' she was saying, 'how I have to engage local people to dust and clean and make beds, get in sufficient food to feed an army...'

'I've already apologised twice, Grandmother, and again, I'm sorry. This time it worked out that way. Other times, we know well in advance. Anyway, that part of the house is always kept spotless.'

'How many this time?' she asked.

'Bill Parton, Barry Henderson, George Smythe, plus, of course, Moira, our secretary.' A pause. 'Drusilla Jameson.'

'*She* is coming?' No answer from her grandson. 'I thought you had disentangled yourself from that young woman?'

Terri stared at Brendan, willing him to nod, say yes, anything to deny the meaning implicit in his grandmother's question.

He made a doubtful face. 'It depends——' he pushed away his coffee-cup '—on what you mean by "disentangled".'

He had, Terri reflected with a sadness so intense she could hardly bear it, erected his 'keep out' notice.

The silence was broken by the striking of the grandfather clock in the hall. It was a signal, Terri had been staying there long enough to know, that the meal had ended and the evening had begun.

She pushed away from the table. Her free time had begun, too.

'Will you please excuse me?' she requested, to which Mrs Stewart replied, as she always did,

'Of course, dear. But,' she added with a smile as Terri reached the door, 'no rowing across that inlet, now.'

Terri laughed, pretending to be upset. 'Never again, Mrs Stewart? There seems to be so much over there to explore and discover.'

'What is there in my cottage...' her grandson's voice held a grating note as he addressed her, rising also '...that you have not already seen, that draws you back to it? What's this "discovery" you want to make over there?'

I could tell him, Terri thought, that it's the atmosphere of the place that touches me, makes me want to absorb it so that I can write about it more convincingly. But she knew that on no account could she tell him that. It would mean revealing her secret—that she was compiling a plot for a story which her journalist sister had commissioned from her. Anyway, even if she did tell him, he would only laugh and dismiss it as feminine nonsense.

His narrowed, suspicious gaze brought a frown to her face. 'I was only joking,' she replied in what was, she hoped, a throw-away manner.

In her room, she took out her reporter's notebook and flipped the pages. She felt within her the urge to begin the story, but where should she start? She sat on the cushioned window-seat and gazed across the inlet, as smooth and innocent now as last night it had been rough and daunting.

Brendan's cottage, white-washed as its outer walls were, glowed in the fading light. Behind it the ridged and rocky mountains rose, adding their darkening bulk to the advancing night.

Might someone over there, her imagination suggested, be wandering round the outside, as she had done, looking for a way in? She scribbled a few lines. Someone who wanted access to that room she had crept into that morning, while Brendan had taken Snippet for a walk?

The story, she thought delightedly, was writing itself. Her hand trembled just a little in its efforts to keep up with the words her brain was feeding to it. She was back inside that cottage, the shadows growing longer, the lights flickering as the generator waxed and waned in its output...

A movement tore a gasp from her throat. It was the sound of the door of her bedroom closing. Her swinging glance showed her that Brendan stood there, his arms folded, his stance belligerent.

She slammed her notepad shut, sliding the pencil into the coiled wire that held the pages together. Her hasty actions drew his glance and she cursed herself for betraying such confusion at his sudden appearance.

He strolled towards her, pausing a few feet distant. Her instinct was to look for a hiding place for her notebook, to slide it beneath the cushion on which she sat. Instead, she held it tightly to her chest.

'Why so secretive, Miss Butler?' There it was again, that accusation in his voice and eyes. His switch to formality puzzled her. 'What's so top secret about the words you were writing that you're actually afraid that I might ask to see them?'

'No.' She shook her head a little too fiercely. 'I'm not afraid.'

His hand came out. 'So——?'

'I'm sorry, but I can't allow you to read it. I mean...'

She pressed it closer to her and he seemed inordinately annoyed at the action. Should I tell him the truth? she wondered. Of course not, an inner voice cautioned. First, it's nothing whatsoever to do with him; second, she remembered her sister's cautionary words. 'Never tell,' she'd advised. 'Talk about it and it's worked itself out of your system.'

Anyway, she argued silently, I might never get around to completing the story, which would mean I'd look stupid in his eyes. And, for some reason she would not let herself even attempt to define, she wanted to remain high in this man's regard.

His brooding expression slowly ebbed, giving place to a kind of dismissive resignation. He wandered to the bookcase which Mrs Stewart had provided, apparently as amused as his grandmother had been at the number of volumes, both fiction and non-fiction, that Terri had brought with her.

He inspected the titles as she had done in his room across the inlet, also, like Terri, withdrawing some of the volumes. Replacing them, he turned, hands thrust into his trouser pockets, his gaze thoughtful as it dwelt on her. He wandered across, looking down at her.

She had managed furtively to push her notebook on to the windowsill behind the heavy curtain, but the fact that her hands were now empty did not, she was sure, escape his notice.

'Some of those books,' he said at last, 'are textbooks. Some man has written his name in them. Leslie Cowley. Boyfriend, current or ex?'

'Neither. My sister's husband. He's got a scientific background, like you.'

'Which company does he work for?'

Not, she noticed, What's his job?

'A publishing company. Like my sister, he's a journalist. He's the editor of a scientific magazine.' She smiled. 'Always wants to be first with the latest discoveries, you know?'

Why, she wondered, had his expression closed down?

He said nothing, walking away, then coming back. 'So you're not just a pretty face.'

'What do you mean?' She began to feel oddly guilty. She knew that she had done nothing wrong, yet in his book it seemed she had.

He nodded towards the bookshelves. 'Physics and mathematics. Chemistry.'

Relief began to undo the knots into which her insides had tied themselves. 'I used them to pass my school exams. My parents wanted me to go on to higher education. So did my brother-in-law, which is why he lent me his books, to encourage me. But my father lost his job, so I had to find work instead to help them financially.'

'The grades you gained in your exams were good enough to enable you to go on to university if you'd been able to?'

'They were, yes.' Terri frowned, unable to understand where his questioning was leading. 'Why?'

He was so long in answering that she tried to read his expression, but darkness had stolen most of the light. When his hand came out, inviting her to put hers into it, she remembered the way his had felt in the night, the way it had touched her skin—it had started to tingle at the mere memory—threatening, as it had then, to break through her carefully constructed defences.

She could not prevent her hand from accepting the invitation of his. It felt cool and strong, causing a shock to shoot along her arm.

'So you speak my language, Terri Butler.'

She was unable to move for astonishment. 'But chemistry and biochemistry aren't the same, are they?' Her hand shook free of his and she jumped up, making for the dictionary, returning to the window-seat and using the last of the light to read by.

'Biochemistry,' she said, 'is a study of the chemical processes of living organisms. Whereas...' Turning the pages, she read out, 'Chemistry's defined as "the study of the elements and the reactions they undergo"——'

'I know what chemistry is,' he broke in irritatedly.

And so do I, she thought.

Every time he came into her line of sight, let alone the same room, she felt the chemistry of him mixing with hers. One day, she was certain, there would be an almighty explosion...

'Anyway...' she was on the defensive and did not know why '... I only took all those subjects to a relatively low level.'

Replacing the dictionary, she turned, only to discover that Brendan had taken her place on the window-seat. It had grown dark and as she drew level with one of the table lamps she reached out to switch it on, trying at the same time to decide whether to join him, or choose another place to sit.

The choice was made for her. His hand came out, catching her wrist and pulling her down beside him.

'Stop,' he said between snapping teeth, 'being so bloody elusive.'

At which his arms pulled her to him, his mouth coming down to take hers over, pressing back her head. Their thighs made contact, their hips likewise and, as if this fired his desire even more, he moved her bodily on to his lap.

The contact acted like dynamite on her reflexes and she felt a throb low down. Her arms had wound themselves around his neck and her lips, too, decided to join in the fun.

He put her from him at last, looking her over, eyes hooded. 'That's better,' he commented, his arm supporting her as she half lay in his arms. 'Much better.'

It isn't better, she wanted to cry, it's the very opposite. The more you kiss me, the more I feel the hardness of your body, the strength of your arms, the more under your spell I fall. Too late, you've already fallen, and hard, a voice prodded inside her head. This man's in your system, and there he'll stay.

His eyes were busy inspecting her patterned, hip-length woollen sweater. 'You've a man walking all around you,' he commented with a taut smile.

He traced the design, his fingertip pressing the figure of the kilted dancing Highlander which alternated with the shape of bagpipes, pressing against her, against her hips, her waist, then, devastatingly, against her breasts, wherever the pattern led, in fact, causing her to writhe.

'Don't,' he commanded through clenched teeth, 'do that unless you want me to make love to you, the love you deprived me of last night, not to mention this morning.'

'S-stop trying to s-seduce me, then,' she heard herself pleading. 'And anyway, you have no right to demand nor even to ask *anything* of me.'

'No?' He slid her to her feet, joining her, pulling her against him, his hand sliding inside her blouse and finding the sensitive peaks, showing no mercy even as she moaned and pleaded with him to stop.

Her mouth, loving the feel of his, wanted more and more and it was only when a sharp bark and a flurry of fur wrapped around her legs that she came down to earth and broke away. Her heart was pounding, her legs unsteady, and it was as much out of the need to find support as the wish to play with the dog that she allowed her knees to give way and find a place on the tufted carpet.

There came a smothered curse from Brendan as Snippet scurried round his feet. The dog dropped the lead from his teeth, squatted and gazed expectantly up at him.

'He's saying "walk",' Terri managed, rising but finding herself unable to meet Brendan's eyes.

'You don't say,' came from him sarcastically as he bent to pick up the dog's lead, slapping it against his leg. 'I swear that this,' he said, gesturing to the dog, 'is my grandmother's doing. Are you sure,' he addressed Snippet, 'that there isn't a note tucked into your collar saying, Remember my warning, Grandson. Hands off my secretary, or else——?'

Snippet panted, tongue lolling, while Terri laughed, her eyes shining, tugging her sweater back into place.

'OK, so I'll heed my grandmother's caution...' a telling pause ' . . . this time.'

'Every time,' Terri declared heatedly. 'I don't want to lose my job.' Or you, she tacked on silently.

At the door, he turned. 'Every time? Oh, no, lady. What do you think I'm made of—granite, like the rocks around us? I'm a normal man——'

'Not,' she almost choked, anger mixing with a strange desperation, 'without love.'

'*Love*? You believe that exists, in this day and age? How naïve can you get?'

'At least I'm not a cynic, like you,' she retaliated. 'There has to be some—well, catalyst at some point that changes mere—mere lust to love?'

Her voice rose uncertainly, although she had intended to make a telling statement.

'Catalyst...ah,' he said mockingly, 'now she's talking like a chemist. That I understand. Take it from me...'

He took a few steps back into the room, a stark intensity in his eyes. 'No such spontaneous change exists where most intimate relations are concerned.'

'Call it *lovemaking*,' she insisted, hearing a note of anguish in her own voice.

'Call it what you will, I still maintain,' he said, harshly now, 'that there's no *love* about it.'

'There is!' She wanted to cling to her dreams.

'You . . .' he returned to the door, fixing the lead to the collar of an unusually patient Snippet '. . . have a lot of growing up to do.'

She ran to throw at his retreating figure, 'Becoming cynical isn't growing up. So you were let down once. Lucky you. Some men are let down many times.'

At the top of the stairs, he faced her. 'Oh, yes? With *you* being the cause of one of those let-downs with some unfortunate man?'

They were, she knew, engaged in a discussion that went far deeper than a mere disagreement. She felt a driving desperation to alter his mind, to prove to him that *she* wouldn't let a man down once she'd let him near to her, given to him all she had to give.

'No!' There were tears in her voice now. '*I* was the one who was let down, I——' her finger hit her chest '—I the woman, the *unfortunate* woman.'

He looked at her curiously, starting to speak but changing his mind, restraining Snippet who could not wait to get down the stairs.

For some time afterwards, Terri sat on the window-seat, watching the hills fade to mere outlines, then disappear altogether.

She *was* desperate, she told herself, desperate to get her employer's grandson out of her thoughts, to stop her heart from pounding whenever she saw him, to walk the other way whenever his hand, let alone his lips, reached out to touch her. It wouldn't just be an uphill task, she knew that. It would be like climbing Everest in bare feet, without ropes, without oxygen even . . .

Two days later, Terri found herself with time on her hands. She had finished the work which Mrs Stewart had given her. When she had taken it to her employer's room for her signature, she had, while waiting, stared through the window.

A sigh had escaped her. Mrs Stewart, hearing it, had queried, 'Are you looking for my grandson?'

The question had jolted Terri into swinging round, full of denial. Surely Mrs Stewart hadn't guessed her secret?

'It would be perfectly natural,' Christiana had admitted. 'Ever since you came nearly four weeks ago I have been worried about your not meeting others of your own age. Which, my dear, is why I welcomed Brendan's arrival on the scene.'

Terri had sighed again, silently this time, relieved that her secret was safe.

'Just as long as his masculinity,' Mrs Stewart had added with a smile, 'and, old as I am, I can understand his mind and his instincts, is kept under very strict control where you're concerned. Other women,' she'd said with a delicate lift of the shoulders, 'the liberties they allow him to take, that is up to them—and him. But you . . .'

It was as well, Terri had thought, that Mrs Stewart hadn't been able to see the inward flinch as jealousy of the most alarming kind had hit her at the picture her words had conjured up . . . of Brendan looking at another woman as he had looked at her as she'd occupied half his bed the other night; of Brendan's hooded eyes as he'd lifted his head from kissing her in her room two days before.

'It does seem some time since I've seen him around,' she had agreed, forcing a note of casualness into her voice.

'Preparing for this seminar of his, probably,' Christiana had commented. 'Busy contacting local people who are only too glad to help with the catering and the domestic side of things. Have you seen the extension where they'll be congregating?'

Terri had shaken her head.

'You must have a look some time. It was built for use as a school, but the young children left one by one as their parents moved away.' She had shaken her head sadly. 'I miss their voices, their sweet singing, the happy eagerness in their eyes.' It was Mrs Stewart's turn to sigh. 'I remember Brendan as a small child. How I've wished,' she'd said with a rueful smile, 'that young people now were as keen to marry——' her smile was wistful now '—for love, of course, and reproduce themselves as they were in my younger days.' A longer pause. 'A little Brendan running around would fill my life to the brim with great-grandmotherly delight!'

No commitment, Brendan had said—'bliss without the wedded'. Therefore no children... It hurt Terri physically to recall Brendan's words.

Mrs Stewart's invitation came back to Terri now. She could, she reflected, make some more notes for her story but, her spirits being lower than usual, she felt that the necessary inspiration was lacking.

Or she could take Snippet for a walk. Going in search of him, she found him dozing in the kitchen at Harvey's side. He did not even wake up when she entered.

Harvey smiled. 'He's too busy chasing his enemies in his dreams to go chasing after them with you, lassie,' was Harvey's humorous comment and Terri nodded resignedly.

She retreated, knowing deep down the identity of the person she would most have liked to talk to, but there hadn't been a sign of him all day. Probably gone over to his hideaway, she decided. The hills and mountains beckoned, but for once their challenge did not draw her.

So why didn't she take up Mrs Stewart's invitation right now?

Hands in the pockets of her cotton trousers, she wandered around the outside of the house. Approaching the extension, she wondered, with a flash of excitement, whether the entrance, recessed into an open porch, was locked. It was not and as she entered she realised that the inspiration for which she had sought earlier was coming back to life.

There was a lobby with hooks for coats, and lockers for personal possessions. Opening off the entrance area were glass-windowed doors through which she spied desks and chairs, while at the front of the room was a larger desk in front of a blackboard.

Further along was another room, its atmosphere relaxing with its armchairs and settees. In a corner stood a large television set. Plainly a place for letting one's academic hair down, she decided, wandering into a kitchen containing spotlessly clean equipment.

A few doors along she found the computer for which she had searched in Brendan's room across the inlet. There was not just one but, she counted, half a dozen!

'Are you computer literate?'

Terri swung round, eyes flying open. 'That, I suppose,' she retorted, 'is your high-falutin way of asking me if I'm intelligent enough to use a computer.'

He pretended to wince. 'She has sharp claws.' He reached out and took her hand, inspecting her nails. 'Remind me to file them down some time.'

She snatched her hand away, anger overtaken by a much more potent emotion. She'd wanted him never to let that hand go...

'High-falutin,' he echoed her accusing word, 'meaning pompous, pretentious?' He shook his head. '"Computer literate" is a perfectly acceptable term...a scientist's way of talking.'

Sharply she hit back, 'Which means I don't speak your language whatever you may say.'

'It all depends on the language, doesn't it?' His narrowed eyes skated over her. 'Body language, for instance. I think we two could have a prolonged conversation in that. Love talk——'

'You don't believe in love,' she heard herself protest. 'You told me so yourself. Just——'

'Unbridled sex?' he mocked. 'Try me, Miss Butler,' he said softly, moving closer. 'You'd be surprised how *persuasive*, how *tender* I can be.'

Before she could guess his intention, his arms were round her, his mouth smothering any protest she might try to make. But any thought of protesting flew out of the window as she felt her body succumb to his roving hands, the feel of his hips against hers making her legs turn to water.

The sound of a car engine approaching had her stiffening in his embrace. He released her, but taking his time, searching her flushed face, his gaze fixing on her bright gaze.

'Convinced?' he asked huskily.

'Of your practised, *experienced* approach to seduction, yes,' she hit back, smoothing her hair and putting to rights her cotton top which his hand had unaccountably invaded. 'But not of your sincerity, nor of your moral scrupulousness.' She paused. 'Nor of your ability to *love*.'

'Why, you——' His lips curled, his fingers seized her wrist, jerking her to him, but brakes applied at too fast a speed had him throwing away her arm and striding to the entrance door. The kiss, she thought despondently—it was as if it had never happened.

CHAPTER SIX

FIXING chunky beads above the rounded neckline of her peach-coloured silky top, Terri reflected that she had begun to look more like a guest than someone who had agreed, at her employer's request, to help with the drinks at the buffet meal.

It was to be a small affair, Mrs Stewart had informed her. 'We thought it would be a pleasant way to start off the proceedings. One of the lady helpers is unable to come,' Mrs Stewart had added, 'so, my dear, I'm taking advantage of your good nature and asking you to take her place.'

'Gladly,' Terri had told her employer, reflecting silently that Brendan would be there, wouldn't he?

Straightening her cream-coloured cotton skirt, she fixed earrings to match the beads, trying to forget the scene she had witnessed through the window of the computer-room after Brendan had left her.

From a minibus, one by one a line of laughing people had stepped out—four men and two women. One of the women had broken away and progressed—there was no other word for it—towards Brendan with a grace and beauty that had provoked in Terri a tormenting kind of envy.

The owner of those attractions had proceeded to lift her arms to his neck, bestowing on his apparently un-reluctant mouth a kiss which to Terri's desolate gaze was much warmer and had lasted far longer than was normal as a mere greeting.

Sighing now and descending, Terri made her way through an inner communicating door to the extension.

The kitchen was buzzing with activity, its spotless surfaces having disappeared beneath dishes and plates and
whatever else might be considered essential to make the
party go with a swing.

The guests had already assembled, dressed so for-
mally, Terri noticed with amusement, that it would have
gladdened Mrs Stewart's heart had she been there to see
it. She had been invited, she'd told Terri, but had de-
clined her grandson's invitation.

'Drinks first, lassie,' one of the lady helpers remarked
to Terri. 'Their tongues'll be hanging out for a wee drop,
no doubt about that! Take that tray first, will ye?'

Tray held high, Terri eased her way with drawn-in
delicacy through the suited figures, one or two of whom
briefly broke off their conversations to give her a passing,
appreciative glance. Eager hands reached out towards
the filled glasses and as the last of them was taken and
she swung the tray to her side her glance bounced off
the gaze of the party's host. There was a frown in it
which, she felt, boded ill for her.

With a brief excuse, he left the side of the glamorous
woman who had been, until then, holding his undivided
attention.

'What the hell are you doing here?' came Terri's way
as she attempted to make her escape back to the kitchen
for more supplies. 'Not so fast.' Brendan's hand came
out to detain her. 'How did you manage to inveigle your
way into this reception?'

'Inveigle'? Why, she wondered, bewildered, did he
regard everything she did with such suspicion? Well,
she'd play him at his own game.

Hiding the tray behind her back, she answered, 'To
spy on you, that's why. It's what you as good as accused
me of the other day, isn't it? At every opportunity, in
fact?'

'By all that's wonderful! It's Terri Butler, isn't it?'
The voice, she realised, belonged to a tall young man

with dark, flat-combed hair and black-framed spectacles. His glass was upraised as if to toast the girl he had addressed. 'To coin a phrase, Terri,' he went on, 'fancy meeting you. And here, of all places, among the wild men of Scotland.' He glanced obliquely at his host, then edged to Terri's side. 'So how are you? Shh.' His finger went conspiratorially to his mouth. 'How's the girl with the secret mission?'

Terri swallowed a gasp. 'Clive! Clive Keston.' She congratulated herself on her newly acquired ability to simulate pleasure. 'What a strange coincidence.' Why, she wondered with dismay, had the surprise in her voice sounded so hollow?

She glanced with a kind of desperation around the room. An expectant silence had descended. Local dignitaries, invited, Christiana Stewart had confided, out of courtesy, waited smiling for all, as they plainly believed, to be revealed. As, Terri realised, did Brendan's colleagues.

Their host, she noted, her glance bouncing off his tautened features, without doubt shared their anticipation, but minus their tolerant humour. He looked, in fact, she reflected, as if his suspicion of her had been completely vindicated.

She had known immediately what Clive Keston had meant. He'd been referring to the story that her sister had commissioned her to write... Her eyes scanned the waiting audience. She couldn't, she just couldn't tell her precious secret to the world. And how *could* her sister have given that secret away?

'You've seen Madge lately, then?' she countered, realising too late that her question, to hostile, suspecting ears, would probably confirm her evil intent—that she did indeed have a 'mission', that she had a clandestine reason for being there.

It had served its purpose, however, since the assembled company stopped listening. Brendan, Terri noticed with relief, had also turned away, but she knew for certain by his rigid demeanour that his mind was only half on what the fair-skinned, velvet-attired lady at his side was saying. The other half without doubt was on her, Terri's, conversation with his colleague.

'No, not Madge,' Clive was saying. 'I dropped in on your brother-in-law, Leslie. He actually condescended to lever himself out of his editorial chair and treat me to a drink at the nearest pub. Told me you'd got yourself a job in the Scottish Highlands. Couldn't remember where.' He grinned. 'Never guessed I'd bump into you here, though. How's the——?'

Story going... Terri could hear the words before they left his lips.

'Weather been?' she cut in adroitly. 'Windy, wet at times, sunshine now and then.' Her quick glance at Brendan told her that he had overheard and was smiling, tautly, and even reluctantly, at her evasive tactics, but underlying all that, she sensed, he was still angry with her.

'Er-hmm.' Clive cleared his throat and lowered his voice. 'So what's between you and that particular wild man of Scotland?' He nodded towards Brendan, whose attention had been claimed by one of the local dignitaries. 'You his secretary or his——?' He cleared his throat again, even more meaningfully. 'And you've done something to annoy him? Like look at another man?'

'Not his secretary,' Terri told him, ignoring the innuendo. 'Mrs Stewart's. That is, his grandmother's.'

Producing the tray from behind her back, she told him, 'I'm supposed to be helping.' With a falsely bright smiled she added, 'You will excuse me, won't you?'

'You doing anything tonight?'

Clive's question followed her, but she pretended not to hear.

* * *

Terri dined with Mrs Stewart, who then decided to spend
the evening in her room.

'My grandson is fully occupied with his guests and
colleagues,' she informed Terri, rising and accepting the
walking stick from her. 'And,' half under her breath,
'no doubt with that Drusilla woman. If he had half an
eye, or used any of that good Scottish common sense
he was born with——' she progressed to the door with
Terri at her side '—he'd see through her surface attractions, and see her for what she was—a gold-digger...'
She took the stairs slowly. 'My grandson's financial
prospects are excellent, you know; he is my only
heir... and she's an opportunist, too clever—and I do
mean clever—a female without a single redeeming
feature. Thank you, my dear.' She sank into her favourite
chair and looked up with a brilliant smile into Terri's
face. 'I bless the day that you came into my life. Now
off with you, and enjoy your free time.'

As Terri wandered along to her room, she noticed that
Brendan's door was half-open, but not for the world
would she look round it into the room. She did not want
to be caught again in his surveillance trap. He might
have his binoculars trained on the windows, or he might
use the trick again of telephoning his room to test if it
was empty...

Voices and laughter drifted across from the extension.
Half of her wanted to join the after-dinner socialising—
the visitors had dined there, waited on by the temporary
staff—while the other half said acidly, Don't, because
if you do, you'll see the glamorous Drusilla cosying up
to Brendan, while he does nothing at all to resist her
feminine wiles.

On impulse, she pulled on her new zipped jacket and
hurtled down the stairs to the kitchen. As she erupted
into it, Harvey, busy washing the pots and pans, turned
with mild surprise.

'What's up, lassie? The devil at your heels?'

'Just felt I had to take a walk. Oh, no,' she said, frowning down at Snippet, 'he's not asleep again? Come on, lazybones.' She lifted his lead from its hook. 'Walk?'

He was pawing at the door in a flash, tail wagging madly. Laughing, she slammed the kitchen door behind her and raced the dog out through the gate, across the empty road and down to the inlet.

While the dog roamed, seeking new scents, Terri absent-mindedly swung his lead and stared across at Brendan's cottage. In her thoughts she reached out to it, remembering how she had shared his bed.

How many times, she wondered, had Drusilla done the same, down in London, or wherever he lived when away from his grandmother's house? And with how different an outcome!

How she wished now that she had allowed him to break down her barriers that night, to make love to her. How much more easily, she reasoned, could she have fought her rival—her *clever* rival—the beautiful Miss Jameson, armed with the knowledge that his arms had been around *her*, Terri Butler, his mouth taking over her own, his body making her his forever...

It was a fantasy, she reproached herself, a dream. No matter how many times she might have let him love her, there would have been no commitment on his part, no longer-term, *permanent* relationship between them. Hadn't she already been warned by him?

'So this is what you were doing tonight.'

She almost jumped out of her skin.

Clive Keston stood beside her, his glance vaguely reproachful. 'I did ask but you didn't answer.'

'I didn't know myself until a few minutes ago. I just felt the urge... Snippet,' she called, 'here.'

The dog obeyed, but wandered away again.

'How...?' She hesitated, not really wishing to bring the subject up, but she had to know. 'How did you hear about my story?'

'So you know what I was going to ask. Why didn't you answer? You're good, aren't you, at taking verbal evasive action?'

Terri did not smile in response to the joke that was not really a joke, but, curiously, more of a reproach.

'When Leslie and I went back to his office after lunch the other day, your sister Madge had arrived.'

Terri nodded, knowing that Madge often called in on her husband at lunchtimes, the head offices of their respective magazines being only a ten-minute walk away from each other.

'When Madge heard I was coming north to Scotland, she happened to mention that you'd found yourself a job up here. She couldn't remember where, nor the name of your employer.'

This time, Terri did smile. 'Typical vagueness on my sister's part. She's so wrapped up in her work, she forgets things that don't have any connection with it. So she let it slip that she'd suggested I might find a plot for a story up here?' Clive nodded. 'I wish she hadn't. It's a secret. You see...' she doubted if he would '...it's said that once you talk about something you're creating it's out of your system and it's, well, kind of gone. Don't tell anyone, will you?'

He gave an almost disbelieving laugh. 'Not much of a mission, is it? Not much of a secret, either. But since you've asked me to keep mum, I won't tell a soul.'

'Thanks.'

Terri frowned. What was it with everybody who came here? she pondered. Did they all become suspicious of everyone?

There was a pause, in which gulls swooped and cried, then Clive queried, 'Know why we're here?' Another pause followed, during which Snippet ventured into the water, then, finding himself almost drowned by particularly large waves, quickly left it, shaking himself energetically.

'We're on to something.' Clives's voice had lowered. 'I dropped a hint—only a hint, mind—to Leslie. Needless to say, he was on to it at once. Wants to be first to publish it in his magazine. I promised him a scoop, just as soon as we know for certain.'

Terri's heart unaccountably swooped, like the flight of a gull overhead, but without regaining height. Something told her that Clive shouldn't be telling her this. Snippet barked loudly and chased away.

'It's a secret,' Clive confided. *Another* secret? she thought. 'But don't put that into the story you're writing, will you?'

How she wished that Madge hadn't mentioned that story, not to Clive, nor to anyone.

'And Brendan?' she queried. 'Where does he come into all this?'

'He's the project leader. It's a new drug we're researching into. Initial trials are encouraging. There's a group of us working on it. We've reached a crucial stage. Hence this discussion we're going to have, in a congenial atmosphere, away from the distractions of academia.'

Clive shivered in the stiff breeze. 'You were sensible enough to wear a jacket. I'm a stranger to the Scottish climate. I need another layer. Coming?' He gestured towards the house.

There was a sharp smothered bark and Terri realised she had not seen Snippet for a while.

'Not yet.' She smiled. 'Must find the dog and take him for the walk I promised him.'

Clive saluted in acknowledgement and crossed the road, making for the house. There came another sharp, cut-off bark and Terri grew alarmed, looking about her in the gathering darkness. Was he hurt? she wondered. Had he become caught up in a prickly bush?

Her steps took her quickly back across the road and in the direction from which the barks had come. Now there was the sound of a scuffle and she started to run.

Somebody was trying to steal him and he was struggling for his freedom!

Skidding round a corner of the house, she saw the outline of a man. His blouson jacket bulged in front and, to her amazement, the bulge moved.

'Snippet,' she shrieked, throwing herself at the man who, she told herself, was trying to spirit the dog away. 'Come, Snippet, bite him, scratch him!'

There came a squeal and, convinced that the man was hurting the animal, she threw herself at him. Which, she realised at once, was the wrong thing to do, because it would have been Snippet who had taken the full force of the impact.

Seconds before her body made contact with that of the thief, Snippet leapt mightily from above the jacket's zipped opening, landing on his feet and barking with a deafening insistence. Warning her? Terri wondered hazily, realising that it was she now who was imprisoned, having taken the place of the dog in the man's embrace.

If that, she thought, still dizzy with the impact, was the word to describe the bear-clutch with which those arms of muscled steel, as her somewhat disordered mind now thought of them, imprisoned her.

She tried to pull away to see the man's face, but even if she had been able to it would, she realised, have been too dark to take note of his features.

It was his voice that told her who it was, deep and clipped.

'So the bait worked.'

'It's you,' she breathed, although even that was an effort. 'I should have known. Only Brendan Stewart would use a helpless animal to trap a woman he wanted.'

Easily he stilled her struggles, his breath fanning her mouth as he talked down at her, her chin caught, as it was, against his wool-covered chest, her face therefore upturned towards his.

'Let us, shall we, analyse that statement?'

'True to form,' she managed somehow to bite back, although it hurt her chin to talk. 'Clinical, objective, coldly scientific, no matter what the circumstances.'

He moved against her and she had to place her feminine responses under a very tight rein.

'You'd prefer me,' he queried silkily, 'to be more *emotional, subjective,* warmly personal?'

'For—for heaven's sake.' Her mouth was dry. 'W-what were you saying?' Anything to bring his mind back to its objectivity.

'A helpless animal?' he pursued the subject. 'That creature that's snapping at our feet and ruining our hearing by its noise, *helpless*? And *trap* a woman? You really think I need to use devious means to *pull* a member of the opposite sex?'

'*You* called hiding Snippet "a bait",' she pointed out, liking more and more the feel of his chest against her cheek.

'For my own reasons, lady, purely *objective* reasons, with not even a hint of emotion or sensual needs involved. And to continue...' He turned her into a more comfortable—too comfortable, she reflected hazily—position, his arms going round her, his lips a mere whisper from hers. 'A woman I *wanted*? Oh, yes...' his voice was husky now '...you're so right. I *want* you, Terri Butler, but—be honest with me—I'd have no need to *trap* you, would I? Because you want me as much as I want you. And one day, my lovely deceiver, I'll have you.'

His mouth came down before she could pose her question... Deceiver? What do you mean? His lips were punishing and ruthless, drawing from her a response that both delighted and frightened her, telling him, she realised, without any doubt, that he attracted her, and that she wanted him every bit as much as he had claimed that he wanted her.

He lifted his head at last, putting her from him with a force that almost made her lose her balance. 'You were having an interesting discussion with Keston?' he clipped. 'He was imparting information that you'll no doubt put into that notebook of yours the minute you go back to your room?'

Frowning, she shook her head. 'Discussion? Information? What do you mean? The things I write in my notebook, they're...' Alarm bells shrieked their customary warning: Don't tell, don't tell.

'Yes?'

She wished she could touch him, smooth away the frown which the light emanating from the half-moon shining overhead revealed to her.

'The notes I'm making are purely personal, descriptions of—the hills,' she invented, 'the mountains, the—the beauty that's everywhere around us.'

Had she put him off the scent?

'You don't own a camera? You do? So what's wrong with using that to remind you of that beauty?'

Why was he still so suspicious? 'I do take pictures, but—but a camera lens doesn't tell you about the stillness, the scents in the air...'

'How come you're on such familiar terms with Clive Keston?'

The curt question, out of the blue, startled her.

'Familiar?' she queried. 'I wouldn't call it that. I first met him four years ago at Madge and Leslie's wedding. He and Leslie have been friends, or so Madge told me, from their schooldays. They eventually went their own ways.'

'But they kept in touch?'

Terri nodded. 'Leslie opted for magazine journalism, while Clive graduated and stayed on as a lecturer at the university. Or so Leslie told me. Which,' it struck her suddenly, 'must be where you met Clive?'

'You mean in view of the fact that we both work at the university? You've guessed right.' He seemed to be waiting for more.

'I met Clive after that,' Terri enlarged, 'at the occasional party at Madge and Leslie's home. That's about it.' With a quick smile she asked, 'Disappointed, are you, that no intrigue can be read into that?'

His face was in shadow, but she sensed the flicker of a smile.

'Clive told me, by the way, why you were here, all of you. Also that you're doing research on a new drug; that you've reached a critical stage and want to talk about it. As a team.'

His head lifted sharply. No smile now, but a thrust of the jaw signified something more than irritation.

A series of angry yelps, followed by a small, furry form hurling itself at her legs, cut across the tension that had become almost tangible between them.

'Snippet's annoyed with me,' she offered tentatively to the taut male form in front of her as a cloud passed across the moon. Had it been only a few minutes ago that she had been pressed close against that body, head back, lips taken into the keeping of that hard mouth? 'I'd better take him for the walk I promised him.'

Bending, she fixed the lead to the dog's collar. 'Sorry, Snippet,' she said, 'but you can't go wandering off on your own into the darkness.' He proceeded to strain at the leash, pulling her with him.

'Don't go far.'

The clipped instruction followed her, acting like a challenge. She would not take orders from him!

Her defiant footsteps took her into the semi-darkness—the moon was some help in telling her where to place her feet. Even faster footsteps made her hurry. They sped past her and their owner seized the scampering dog, tugging at the leash until it fell from her fingers.

Brendan's angry expression took on daunting shadows. 'Are you still so ignorant of the ways of this land that you don't know how mists can descend without warning?' As if on cue, the moon clouded over again. 'You see? Which means that *I* will take this hound for a walk.'

'I—I've taken him for an evening walk before...' She did not know why his anger had brought her close to tears.

'With my grandmother's permission?'

'I didn't see any need to ask it.'

'Harvey didn't warn you?'

'He didn't know.'

'So now *you* know. Come, Snippet.' Together, they disappeared into the darkness.

'Why—why are you so angry?' she called after him.

The merest hesitation in his step plus a half-turn of his head was the only answer he gave.

'Brendan? Brendan, darling.'

He must have still been near enough to have heard Drusilla's silky, faintly reproaching tones from the opened doorway, but he strode resolutely on.

One point for me, Terri thought with a triumphant smile, retracing her steps to the extension. The party still hadn't ended, judging by the laughter and the music. She would, she decided, ask if her help was still needed there.

A small-built young woman with close-cut hair almost bumped into her as, dazzled by the sudden light, Terri stepped through the door.

'Hi. You're Terri? I guessed right, then. We haven't met. I'm Moira, Moira Cunningham. I'm attached to that lot in there.'

'Hi. I didn't see you get out of the minibus,' Terri confessed with a smile. 'You're secretary to all these high-minded people?'

'I suppose Brendan mentioned me? High-minded, you said? You must be joking. You should see them when they get the party spirit. Their eyes—they roam... analytically, if you get my meaning...all over you. Their instincts——' She cleared her throat. 'Well, scientists they might be, but physically they're made just like any other man. Sometimes you feel you need four hands to beat them off. And,' she whispered, 'the project leader's no exception. Know who I mean?'

Only too well, Terri thought, nodding even while her heart did a double bump. It really had meant nothing to him, then, she reflected, those kisses, those approaches of his the night he'd slept beside her...

'Moira—hey, Moira,' one of the group, George Smythe, hailed her. 'They're calling your name. Phone call.'

Moira gave a strangled squeak. 'It just has to be Andrew. Andrew Muir, my boyfriend,' she informed Terri breathlessly. 'He lives up here—well, fifty miles away. Long time no love. And do I miss him!' She made a dash.

'Where's Brendan?' The low-pitched, faintly irritated question came not from George, who had disappeared, but from the black-clad woman whose words Brendan had earlier listened to so avidly, and whose lips he had more than tolerated on her arrival.

'I'm not a magician, I haven't made him disappear,' Terri heard herself reply, immediately regretting the tartness of her tone. She could so easily have spoken with a smile, but that was something she couldn't bring herself to do to this woman.

Drusilla approached, a frown only slightly marring her pale good looks. Her outfit was stunning, restrained though it was. It must, Terri reflected, be the shape inside the close-fitting black velvet trousers and beneath the well-tailored matching jacket that gave the outfit its glamour.

'Are you employed here? You work in the kitchens?' Drusilla asked.

Which well and truly puts me in my place, thought Terri ruefully.

'Kitchens? No,' was her half-amused reply. 'I'm one rung higher up the status ladder. I'm Mrs Stewart's secretary, driver, companion.'

Drusilla's brief nod was followed by a deeply reflective stare which unaccountably sent Terri's spirits rocketing. If this woman felt challenged enough to give her this intensive once-over, it must surely mean, mustn't it, that in Drusilla Jameson's eyes she, Terri Butler, constituted a real threat where Brendan Stewart was concerned?

After watching Drusilla enter by the main door, Terri made her way to the rear, stepping into the kitchen and blinking in the bright lights.

'Where's the dog?' Harvey asked anxiously.

'Gone walkies with the master of the house.'

Harvey allowed himself a smile. 'Worried about ye, was he, in the darkness?'

'No,' came her unequivocal response, 'worried about the dog.'

This time, Harvey went so far as to laugh.

The door was flung wide and a ball of fur shot in, released from the restraint of the lead. He made for the heat of the closed-in stove, turning once or twice, then settling down to luxuriate in its warmth.

'Out, hound,' the master of the house ordered, finger pointing to the partly opened connecting door to the main part of the house. The dog rose, head and tail down, reluctantly obeying. 'No animals allowed in the kitchen,' Brendan's directive followed him. 'This isn't the living-room in my cottage.'

His cottage. Terri's eyes flew to Brendan's as his narrowed gaze swung her way. Was he remembering, too?

Removing his jacket, he hung it behind the door. It was, she realised with a jolt, the one that she had borrowed from him before they had even met.

'What is my grandmother's secretary-driver doing in here?' came Brendan's crisp tones.

'You asked me that earlier this evening,' she retorted, 'and I told you why. To *spy* on you. That's what you're convinced I'm doing, isn't it?' At once she regretted her words, which hung on the air.

Busy hands faltered and stopped, breaths were held, then released, work resuming. So everyone was shocked at the way she, a mere employee, had spoken to the master of the house? They didn't know, did they, that she'd shared his bed, felt his mouth take over hers, given him back kiss for kiss?

'I'm sorry,' she whispered. 'I didn't mean it. You know that, don't you?'

His face was a mask, his eyes telling her that her apology had had no effect.

'I don't even believe that there's anything to spy on you about!' she tried to joke. But it was plain that her effort to conciliate and appease had failed.

Turning to Harvey, she asked, 'Is my help still needed in there?'

'They won't stop drinking, lassie,' Harvey answered, indicating a tray laden with filled glasses. 'They're having a ball.'

'A highball, more like it,' came a lady helper's voice from the depths of the dishwasher.

Amid laughter, Terri lifted the tray, informing Brendan in her politest tone, 'Your grandmother asked me to help out as a special favour.'

'Wee Ginny couldn't come,' Terri heard Harvey explain as she held the tray aloft, easing between the chattering guests.

'Brendan!' Drusilla's hand extended past her towards the man emerging from the kitchen. 'Come, join us,

darling. I've missed you so. Besides, we haven't finished
our very important discussion yet, have we?'

Returning to the kitchen with the empty tray, Terri
wondered exactly which form that so-called 'very important discussion' would take. It didn't need very
much imagination, she reflected disconsolately, to guess
the answer.

CHAPTER SEVEN

TERRI chose the table in the window because it gave the best light. Taking out her notebook, she turned the pages, skimming through them.

She breathed in the coffee's aroma as the waitress lowered the cup in front of her. Smiling her thanks, she returned to her notes. A little over an hour stretched before her and she wanted to use that time to add a few ideas to those she had already scribbled down.

'Don't come for me too soon,' had been her employer's instructions. 'Nor too late, Terri. My good friend Annie Macfarlane and I get on well together, because we understand each other. She is a stickler for keeping to a timetable, as indeed, as you must know by now, I am. My timetable this morning is to take coffee with Annie for one hour, ten minutes.'

Consequently, having followed in her employer's still agile footsteps round the shops, Terri had checked her watch against that of Mrs Stewart. After escorting her employer from the car to a smartly painted front door, she had seen her into her friend's house.

If only, Terri thought now, pencil hovering, I could conjure up a storyline out of all these ideas. Putting down the pencil, she lifted her cup and drank, noting with a shock over the rim of it that someone was staring in at her, finger tapping the glass.

The 'someone' was male, and her heart did a lover's leap until disappointment made it plunge into the proverbial yawning chasm. How could she have thought that the man might be Brendan?

'Hi,' said Clive, entering. 'May I?' Taking her agreement for granted, he seated himself opposite her, ordering coffee from the waitress who appeared at his side. 'You don't mind, do you?'

'All the same if I did,' was Terri's answer, a forced smile lifting the drooping corners of her mouth. 'Why aren't you working this morning?'

'We're all supposed to be at the desks in our rooms sorting through our notes and writing presentations to be assessed and discussed by our fellow researchers.' He smiled. 'I'm not playing truant, if that's what you're thinking. I did mine last night.'

'Oh, good for you! You aiming to be teacher's pet?' she joked. 'Ingratiating yourself with the team leader?'

'Brendan Stewart?' He made a face. 'He and I aren't on the same wavelength most of the time. And *teacher's* pet?' His hand extended across the table, covering hers. 'I'd rather be your pet.'

Terri slid her hand from beneath his, quelling the urge to rub it clean. She made a play of flipping the cover of her notebook back into place, then realised what a mistake she had made in drawing his attention to it.

'The masterpiece?' He reached out to take the notebook. 'The very secret blockbuster-to-be?'

'Just a story, a short story.' She tried to wrestle the book from his fingers but he won, slowly turning the pages, then shaking his head.

'Either it's in your personal shorthand, or a foreign language.'

He handed it back and she took it eagerly, relieved that her scrawl had defeated him. She pushed it into her bag and finished her coffee, glancing at her watch. Fifteen minutes to go before collecting her employer. She could, she supposed, excuse herself right now, go to the rest-room...

'Well, look who's watching us. The leader of the team himself. There, across the road.'

Terri looked, her heart bumping. He was indeed watching them, lounging, hands in pockets, head slightly down, against the window of the hairdresser's directly opposite.

'So——' She wished she had some coffee left with which to moisten her parched mouth. 'So Brendan Stewart's playing truant, too.'

Her strained joke made Clive laugh. 'You notice it's a ladies' hairdresser's?'

'I know. I have my hair done there, and I take Mrs Stewart there, too.'

'Bet you a million dollars it's not his granny he's waiting for.'

Terri knew that. 'So who——?'

'Come on, Sherlock Holmes, concentrate.'

'Drusilla?' Had there been any need to gasp the name?

'The very same. Brendan parked his car, quite by chance, next to mine. Drusilla looked as if she'd licked the cream.'

The grandfather clock in the corner struck the quarter hour and Terri gasped again. Gathering her bag, she pushed back the chair.

'Must fly or I'll lose my job. Eleven-thirty on the dot, Mrs Stewart said, and she meant it.' She gave him a quick smile. 'Thanks for your company, Clive. Oh,' she said, pausing guiltily, 'I've forgotten to pay.'

'That's OK, I'll settle.' He stood, but did not follow her. 'Let's make a habit of it, shall we?'

She was out of the door before she could think up a suitably worded brush-off. Her eyes flicked anxiously across the road, but Brendan was welcoming the return of his girlfriend, her looks even more enhanced by the new hairstyle she had chosen. She was standing on her toes in front of him so that he could inhale the scent of her freshly shampooed hair. Gritting her teeth at the provocative little tableau, Terri made for the car park, which, she told herself, she couldn't reach fast enough.

* * *

'Don't address a single word to me,' Mrs Stewart ordered from the rear seat. 'I have a very important decision to make. Please——' her hand waved '—turn on the music if you wish.'

Which Terri proceeded to do, trying at the same time to argue away the strange sense of foreboding that had descended on her at her employer's words. The music, emotionally moving as it was, only served to intensify the sense of dread that somehow her life was on the brink of change.

She went as usual to help Mrs Stewart from the car, but this time, to her surprise, a determined hand waved her away.

'I'm quite capable, my dear,' Christiana Stewart declared, 'of emerging from this vehicle—from *any* vehicle—without undue assistance. You understand?' A smile softened the implied reprimand.

Terri nodded, even though she in fact did not understand. Mrs Stewart did indeed emerge unassisted from the car, and with a sprightliness which almost drew a gasp from her astonished employee. She did, however, accept the walking stick, although using it only lightly, as if she did not really require its support.

Something had happened at Annie Macfarlane's house, Terri decided in some bewilderment, to alter Mrs Stewart's entire attitude, not just to life, but to her age, and even to her infirmities, of which—and even she could not deny it—she had a few.

'Take me,' Christiana commanded over her shoulder as they entered the house, 'to my private sitting-room. No——' a hand kept Terri a few steps away '—I am perfectly able to go there myself.' And go there she did, straight-backed and firm-footed, on her own. She turned, making a concession. 'You may come in, my dear, and arrange the cushions behind me as you usually do.'

Relieved that her attentions were still needed, if only in respect of providing comfort, Terri did as she had been told. Standing back, she did not venture to do more unless instructed to do so.

Settling back with a sigh, Christiana linked her hands in her short lap.

'Will you excuse me, Mrs Stewart,' Terri said, 'while I go and put the car away?'

Christiana nodded. 'After which, will you come back here, please?'

Terri was closing the garage doors when a taxi chugged into the drive. From the direction of the extension, a short figure dashed past her.

'Hi,' Moira called, swinging her zipped bag into the taxi, then throwing herself in behind it.

'Enjoy your shopping spree,' Terri answered with a wave.

Moira shook her head and shouted something from the lowered window, but the taxi's engine was revving and Terri could not catch the words.

Mrs Stewart greeted her return with yet another bright smile. 'Thank you, Terri, for your silence on the journey home. It helped me come to a decision.' There was a pause, then, as if that decision had been momentous, Mrs Stewart declared, 'I shall go.'

Apprehension took the colour from Terri's face. *I* shall go, not *we*? So she had been right, earlier, to be worried about her own future? Forcing a smile, Terri enquired in a whisper, 'Go where, Mrs Stewart?'

The door, which had been ajar, swung wide. On seeing Terri, Brendan paused, then proceeded slowly into the room to stand beside her. Terri could feel the pull of him even though he was not touching her, and she struggled with her instinct to brush his hand with hers.

'Grandmother,' Brendan's harsh tone grated, 'will you please excuse your secretary——?'

'Why,' Terri broke in, 'what have I done now?' But no one was listening.

'Brendan, listen to me.' Terri had never seen her employer's eyes shine so brightly. 'I am taking a holiday. It will be a long one, and the ground I shall cover will be fairly extensive.'

There it was again, that *I*, Terri noticed.

'And?' Brendan seemed willing to reserve judgement.

'Have no fear, Brendan, I shall not be alone.'

'Oh?' Her grandson's eyes swung to Terri. 'You think this girl is capable of looking after you——?'

'Terri? *She* will not be accompanying me.' Another pause for effect. 'I shall be going with my great friend, Annie—Annie Macfarlane. This morning, Terri drove me into the town——'

Brendan's eyes settled reminiscently, but with no kindliness, on the young woman in question.

'—and I had coffee with Annie, which was when she put her holiday plan to me.'

'Holiday plan? *Annie*? She's seventy-five if she's a day.'

'Your calculations are four years out, dear. She's seventy-nine, and, I agree, she looks younger. And you haven't asked me yet where we shall be going. Well, I'll tell you. To Canada. We have it all planned. We will drive across——'

'*Drive*?'

'Calm your fears, Grandson. We shall be hiring a car and a driver. It won't be cheap, but we can both afford a little luxury like that.'

'Suppose——' Brendan ran tensed fingers through his hair. 'Grandmother,' he breathed deliberately slowly, 'have you forgotten *your* age?'

'Indeed I have not. Some people get old early, some people stay young much longer, whatever age they might be. So much of it is in the mind, my dear. I feel young inside, even though I am in my mid-eighties, which, these days, for some lucky people, is nothing, really.'

'*Nothing*? And you consider that Annie, at seventy-nine, will be capable of looking after you? If you should need it,' he tacked on hastily.

'Annie has a constitution like a horse,' his grandmother stated blandly.

'But you——' With his hands on the arms of his grandmother's chair, he leaned over her. 'Grandmother...' His voice had softened almost to a whisper, and Terri felt her feelings for him well up and overflow... this was a side of him she had never seen, a side she—yes, she *loved*; *every* side of him she *loved*. And yes, she loved *him*, as she had never loved before...

'Grandmother,' Brendan was saying, 'you are all the family I have. This idea of Annie's is crazy. For heaven's sake, don't go.'

Her hand rested on his. 'Brendan...' Terri heard the quaver in her voice '... one day you will have a family of your own. I won't always be here, Grandson.' She seemed to need a steadying breath. 'I want to make the most of the rest of my life, however short or long it may be. You *must* try to understand.'

He straightened, thrusting his hands into his jeans pockets. Slowly, he turned to Terri. 'Do you think,' he asked, 'that my grandmother's constitution is strong enough to endure this crazy journey?'

Terri looked at him, at his grandmother, then through the window to the hills beyond. She wished she knew the answer. 'I—I honestly think that if the spirit is strong enough it will carry anyone through any—any endurance test.'

'And you think my grandmother's is?'

'I do. No doubt about that.'

'Well said, my dear,' Mrs Stewart responded happily. 'Brendan, the world doesn't exist only for the young to enjoy. Annie and I will merely be catching up on what we missed as young women through being born into a less tolerant, far less advantaged era. You understand?'

Brendan seemed about to capitulate when the telephone rang. Out of habit, Terri answered, her eyes lifting to Brendan. 'Yes, Miss Jameson, Harvey was right. He's here.' She handed the receiver over. 'For you.'

He nodded, accepting the receiver. 'Drusilla?' He listened, his whole demeanour stiffening. 'What do you mean, Moira's gone? A note? Her boyfriend's mother is ill? They live fifty miles away? They need her?' He swore under his breath. 'For God's sake, *we* need her. Who else among us has secretarial experience? OK.' His voice softened a fraction. 'Not your fault. We'll have to hire someone from an agency, I suppose. Although I hesitate... OK, leave it with me, will you?'

'There,' said Mrs Stewart happily, 'is the answer.' Her finger pointed. '*My* secretary. I must admit I was worried about her employment here in my absence, very worried.'

Terri nodded, having thought about her employment from the moment her employer had stated, 'I shall go.'

Her hopeful eyes swung to Brendan, saw the frown, the lack of encouragement... Well, she couldn't expect bed-sharing and kisses to count towards a job reference, could she?

'Don't worry about me, Mrs Stewart,' she declared, adding with far more confidence than she felt, 'I'll go back to London; I'll soon find another job.'

'That's the trouble,' Mrs Stewart took her up. 'I want you to stay. I shall need you when I return from my vacation. Unless... ?' The question was in her eyes.

'I want to leave here?' Miserably Terri shook her head. Not just here, she wanted to add. The thought of leaving your grandson, the man my foolish heart has given itself to, is shredding my emotions.

'There you are, Brendan,' Christiana said. 'All you have to do is negotiate her salary with her——'

'Grandmother, will you leave this to me?'

Happily, Christiana nodded. 'Away with you. Use the office, if you like.'

'Miss Butler?' Eyebrows lifted coolly, an impersonal arm indicated the door.

Face to face with him in the office, Terri found him no less intimidating.

'Don't say it, Dr Stewart.' She had recently discovered that he, like most of the others in his team, had a Ph.D. in his subject. 'You don't want to offer me Moira's position, even temporarily.' Her shoulders lifted in a gesture that was meant to be dismissive, but which only served to reveal forlorn acceptance. 'As soon as your grandmother leaves for her holiday, I'll make arrangements to go.'

'What were you and Clive Keston discussing over coffee?' he cut harshly across her thoughts. 'The progress of your "secret mission"?'

So he had remembered Clive's joking, if unguarded comment at the reception?

'There isn't a "secret mission". At least...'

Like an eagle swooping on to its prey, he was on to her hesitant attempt to qualify her statement.

'So, a mission, none the less, with all its connotations.' She shook her head.

'It's all very private. Private to me, I mean. Will you please leave it?'

Should she tell him? Something inside her cried, No.

His expression told her that his suspicions of her were still firmly fixed. She whispered, 'Why don't you trust me?'

His answer was a rigid thrust of his jaw and narrowed eyes. A quick stride and hard fingers gripped her upper arms.

'What were you and Keston discussing so intently over coffee?'

Trying to prise his ruthless fingers from their hold, she prevaricated, 'Just—just ordinary things.'

'Like whether or not he agreed with your notes? Like whether *you* liked his hand over yours?'

He'd seen that much?

'All very *private*, was it?' he persisted. 'Ordinary, everyday things?'

'What,' she challenged, giving up the struggle and gritting her teeth at the pain he was inflicting, 'what *you* were doing was very private, wasn't it? Very domestic and *ordinary*, too, waiting for your girlfriend to come out of the hairdresser's? Anyway...' she wanted to stop, but her anger and, worse, her jealousy wouldn't let her '...why can't I have a private life as well as you?'

She should have stopped. She realised that she had confirmed his suspicion that she, Terri, was on the verge of an affair with one of his colleagues, and one who, inexplicably, he didn't seem to like very much.

'*This* is why, Miss Butler.' He jerked her against him, put his mouth to hers, working at her lips until they parted, allowing him entry and total possession, causing her legs to sag, her heart to pound...and all the rest of her to co-operate totally with his efforts to work on her resistance until it melted completely away.

The fragrance of him! She was hooked on it...it thrust her back to the way his own aroma had clung to the clothes she'd borrowed from him, to the bedclothes she had slid between, to the scent of his skin as he had lain beside her...

When eventually he lifted his head, he found tears welling in her eyes, her bruised lips quivering. 'Why?' he asked hoarsely. 'You hate my guts?'

'You're—you're h-hurting me,' she managed. 'My arms...'

He swore deep down in his throat and slowly eased away his fingers. She swayed with the impact of the pain and he caught her to him, this time with a tenderness that caused her heart to swell with love for him.

With his tongue-tip he licked the teardrops from her cheeks. He dwelt on her features one by one, then groaned, as if fighting some negative emotion within himself, and wrapped his arms around her, moulding her to him.

'Woman, if only I could trust you, if I could believe——'

His kiss this time was fired with passion and masculine need and a kind of anger—plus something else she could not for the life of her put a name to.

The kiss ended at last, and she dragged her arms from around his shoulders, admonishing them for clinging so tightly. 'If only I could trust you', he'd said. It was no good, was it, crying for the moon? Without trust, there could be no love. So what else was there to hope for?

This man, she told herself, already had a lady in his life. A man, Terri supposed, might easily have two. If commitment, if love never came into it, a man could even have half a dozen women . . . but she, Terri Butler, would never be one of them.

'It's no deal, Brendan,' she got out, going to the door, 'and it's no. "If only"'s are no use to me. Sorry. Contact an agency, as you said you would.'

She opened the door, shutting herself out.

'Well,' Christiana enquired that evening, 'is Brendan going to do the sensible thing and accept you as a replacement for the runaway secretary?'

'No, Mrs Stewart,' Terri replied as expressionlessly as possible.

'For heaven's sake, why not? I shall show him your references,' she declared. 'They are locked away in a documents box to which I have the key.'

'He won't be interested. He's going to employ an agency assistant.'

Christiana sighed shortly and turned towards the telephone that stood on a table next to her chair. She stabbed out a number, waited, then exclaimed, 'I didn't bring you up to be a fool, Brendan, who can't see beyond the end of your scientific nose! If you don't employ this perfectly respectable, *trustworthy* young woman, I'll...'

She listened. 'What? Cut you out of my will? Don't be impertinent, young man. You're going to inherit the lot, you know that. Listen, Brendan. I have a whole box full of references on this young lady... Certainly not!' she exploded. 'She has not been putting pressure on *me* to pressurise *you*.'

'Please don't, Mrs Stewart,' Terri pleaded, controlling the tremor in her voice with difficulty.

'There now, young man, you've made her cry. She's gone up to her room. Follow her at once.'

He did not follow her; he did not come. Drying her tears for the tenth time, Terri sat in a chair and surveyed the situation. She would book her train ticket for the long journey south. She would be using it in four days' time, the day after Mrs Stewart departed for her holiday with her old friend Annie.

The telephone next to the bed raised its voice. Brendan? she thought, diving to silence it. He had changed his mind?

'Terri,' Brendan's grandmother said, 'I would like you to come along to my room. Yes, I am aware that it is past my bedtime. However, I have been watching a play on television. I've switched it off because I couldn't concentrate. Five minutes, dear?'

A little breathless, she stood at her employer's bedside. The lady was resplendent in a shell-pink bed-jacket, the collar lined with white fur.

'I couldn't concentrate, dear——' she patted the bed and Terri sank down on it '—because I was so concerned about you. No, listen, please. I was worried about myself also, my own concerns. You see, it occurred to me, thankfully in time, that I could not dispense with your services. In my absence, I shall need them more than ever. Without you, who would take charge of my affairs, deal with the correspondence, pay the bills?'

'Harvey?' Terri ventured with a smile.

Mrs Stewart smiled, too, patting Terri's hand. 'I am very fond of Harvey, dear. He has been in my employ for many years. But no, there is no way I could entrust my affairs to him. So,' she declared with a triumphant smile, 'the problem is solved. You stay here and continue working for me. Do you agree?'

'Oh, yes, Mrs Stewart!' Spontaneously Terri leaned forward and placed a kiss on the peach-soft, faintly lined cheek.

Her employer rested her hand over hers. 'No more tears now, do you hear? Right. You may go. And,' she said with eyes that held the faintest hint of moisture, 'thank you, my dear.'

Terri was not called upon to drive Christiana and Annie to the airport. They were starting as they were going to continue, Christiana said, in style.

For the first time in days, Brendan stood at Terri's side as they waved the travellers off in the taxi they had hired.

Terri was about to turn away when Brendan's hand descended on to her shoulder. 'So, you're staying on here.'

'I am.' Her head went back defiantly. 'And no, I did not "put pressure" on your grandmother, as you suggested the other day, nor did I use persuasive tactics to make her keep me on.'

'Oh, I'd keep you on—in my arms, in my bed. Any time. Any man would.'

'On your terms, of course,' she retorted sarcastically.

'But of course,' he mocked. 'Don't tell me——' he swung her to face him '—that you're actually considering it?'

By taking him up on his outrageous comments instead of protesting, she had, she realised, fallen into his trap.

She tugged free of his hold. 'With no commitment? And only a "thanks for the memory" memo placed in the office out-tray and maybe a cheap gift wrapped in second-hand paper?' It was only when her mind re-played her words back to her that she realised that she was actually bargaining with him!

His arms caught her to him, his chest so near that her head tipped back. 'Which, translated, means that *with* commitment, or the offer of it, and a letter written on scented paper, not to mention an *expensive* gift wrapped in gilt foil, you'd come to me, lie in my arms in my bed, and give me——?'

'Myself? Never!'

'So melodramatic,' he commented huskily, lowering his mouth, 'so self-righteous. Baby...' his breath fanned her lips '...I could carry you to my room and take you here and now. Don't try to deny it.'

If he but knew it, she wasn't able to utter a single word of protest. Her lids lowered as his mouth, his hard, wonderfully familiar mouth, covered hers. Whereupon, to her chagrin, her lips accepted the kiss, drank it like a parched wanderer at a desert oasis, gave it back—and back again.

It was only the mad barking of Snippet, skidding round the corner, that brought her back to earth and lifted her companion's mouth from hers. Between Snippet's teeth was his lead, which he proceeded to drop beside them.

'Harvey's doing,' Brendan growled. 'My grand-mother, in her absence, must have passed her mantle of protector of her secretary's virginity to his keeping.'

'Which means he must have seen us,' Terri declared, agitatedly looking at the watching windows of the main house.

'All the same, I've proved my point,' Brendan stated, putting her from him.

'Do you think so?' she retorted, her emotions tied into knots. 'Never, without trust.'

Snippet was growling, first at Terri's feet, then at Brendan's.

'OK, Snippet,' she sighed, 'you win. We'll go walkies. If I could——' her eyes lifted defiantly to Brendan's '—I'd go walking right out of your life.'

'Oh, yeah?' With a taunting smile, he watched her fix the lead to the dog's collar. 'So prove to me,' he called as she walked away, 'that I can trust you.'

She couldn't because there was no way that she would tell him about her story-writing, only to have him laugh in his high-handed way. She'd show him, she thought, lifting her eyes to the summits around them, one day she'd show him how creatively gifted she was. One day she would prove to him that he could respect *her* intellect as much as he clearly respected and admired that of his glamorous lady friend.

CHAPTER EIGHT

'OUR host's in a foul mood,' Clive confided at dinner the following evening as he shared a table with Terri.

Before Mrs Stewart had left for her holiday, and after consulting with Terri, she had suggested to Harvey that in her absence he might take the opportunity to visit his brother whom he had not seen for some time. On the way, he could return Snippet to her friend Marcia, his owner, who had returned from her holiday abroad.

Harvey had jumped at the idea, assuring his employer that the diversion to deliver the dog to his rightful home would be no trouble at all. So, after making sure that there were sufficient provisions in the house to feed an army, let alone, Terri had laughingly said, to cater for her own reasonably small appetite, Harvey had packed his bags and taken the train to Norfolk.

Despite the bulging contents of the store cupboard and freezer, Terri had opted to join the others for meals. Now she sat with Clive in a room made larger by the folding back of a partition and which, she guessed, had probably served as a hall when the extension had been in use as a school.

'What's happened,' Terri asked, 'to make Brendan's mood so black?'

'To put it succinctly, the non-availability of a person sufficiently intelligent and of high enough integrity to fill the vacant post of secretary.'

Now why, Terri pondered, had her heart leapt at the news? You, she told herself, are the last person he'll come to for help; you know what he thinks of *your* integrity.

'Isn't Moira due back soon?'

'She's quit. Her boyfriend, she says, has proposed, so he's now her fiancé, and she's not willing to leave her future mother-in-law while she needs her help. End of message. None of us has the necessary training to oblige. Beats me——' his glance bounced off her '—why he doesn't ask you.'

She answered with a shrug. How could she explain Brendan's strange suspicions about her when she herself didn't know the reasons behind them?

'Mrs Stewart's affairs keep me reasonably busy, even in her absence,' was her deliberately vague reply.

'You fill the rest of your time with your literary efforts?'

'Maybe.' She wished he wouldn't keep referring to it. 'So the agencies aren't any help in supplying a substitute secretary, in Brendan's opinion?'

'Agency, singular. The others are too far away for their personnel to travel this far. And no one, it seems, is willing to live here for the duration of our stay. By the way, have you heard from your sister lately? How're they doing?'

'I got a card from Madge this morning. They're in New York.'

'Both of them?'

'Both. On their respective businesses, if you know what I mean. When they've finished there, they're taking a long vacation and apparently making for Florida. Then they're heading for San Francisco, where Madge is meeting some people connected with her work. And surprise, surprise,' Terri smiled, 'Leslie's meeting a business acquaintance there, too.'

'Good for them. Mixing business with pleasure. Why not? Hang on while I get us some more coffee. Yes?'

Terri nodded, accepting the fresh cup with a murmur of thanks. Something made her glance at the door. Drusilla was entering, talking to someone over her shoulder. And who else, Terri asked herself cynically, would that someone be but the project leader himself?

His eyes were drawn at once to Terri's, moved to rest on her companion, then swung back narrowly to collide with her defiant stare. Why shouldn't I dine with Clive Keston, she was challenging him, or any other man for that matter? You choose your own dinner companions—except—her gaze faltered and fell—that you almost always choose the same person, the same woman, in fact.

'How would you like to try dictating those notes you keep making?' Clive asked, unaware of the new arrivals. 'I've got a pocket tape recorder you could borrow. You could carry it around with you, talk into it whenever and wherever you feel inspired.'

She was more than conscious of the couple across the room who, having collected their meal from the self-service counter, were sorting out the cutlery.

'I suppose I could try,' Terri responded with a smile, aware of Brendan's eyes on her. 'It'd be fun, even if I turned out to be an ineffective dictator.'

'Right. I don't have it with me, but——' He waited while an obliging lady removed their used dishes. 'Look, will you eat with me tomorrow evening?'

'I'm eating with you now.'

'No. I should have said dine. At a hotel in the town? I'll give you the tape recorder then.'

While the feeling of mistrust of the man sitting opposite had not completely left her, for some reason she could not fathom, she felt less hostility towards him than when they had met a few days earlier.

Again her eyes were drawn to Brendan and his companion who, with wine in their respective glasses, were at that precise moment drinking a toast, holding each other's eyes.

'Why not?' Terri's gaze, injected with a sudden warmth, brightened Clive's expression. He could not know, she thought, that a surge of intense jealousy had been the reason for her eager acceptance of his invitation.

Clive dropped Terri outside the main entrance. He had already invited her back to his room, accepting her refusal with a shrug. By the way he waited, his questioning smile illuminated by the car's interior light, she knew that he was hoping for a similar invitation from her.

'Thanks for the meal,' she said. 'And thanks, also, for the loan of the pocket recorder.' She tapped her pocket into which she had slipped it. 'I'll let you know how I get on.'

If he was disappointed by her failure to ask him in, he hid it well, she thought. He leaned across and took a kiss from her lips. She did not enjoy the sensation, but tolerated it with a smile since he had been good enough to buy her a meal.

She got out, closing the door and wishing him goodnight through the lowered window.

'I don't give up easily,' he warned, preparing to drive round to the car park behind the extension. 'That kiss has made me eager for more.'

Sorry, but you won't get it, she thought. 'Thanks for the compliment,' she said aloud. 'But——'

'No buts. Enjoy your conversation with the recorder, won't you?'

The house seemed empty—*was* empty, she reminded herself as she climbed the stairs to her room. For the first time she was conscious of the silence. It was bedtime, but she felt too strung up to sleep, so she ran a comb through her hair and went down again.

There was no doubt about it—she missed her employer's benevolent reign over the household. And she missed Snippet's skidding paws and eager barks far more than she had ever imagined. Even Harvey's absence left a void she had not reckoned with.

In Mrs Stewart's absence, she had been given the run
of the house. Pouring herself a fruit juice and drinking
it as she went, she found her way into the music-room.
The grand piano stood grandly, living up to its name.
Recliner chairs and long settees invited relaxation of the
body while the mind gloried in the beautiful sounds
emanating from the hi-fi equipment.

After a while, she turned off the music and removed
the pocket recorder from her tailored jacket which she
draped over a chair, pushing off her shoes. Half lying
on one of the three-seater sofas, she started speaking
into the small recorder. Hearing her own voice echoing
in the room's emptiness made her feel self-conscious and
her thoughts would not turn themselves into coherent
words.

Trying again with the same result, she sighed, deciding that she was too tired to think straight. Draining
her glass, she padded across to the hi-fi, finding a
Tchaikovsky recording and operating the equipment.
Music filled the room again as she returned to the sofa
and lay full-length with her hands behind her head.

From nowhere came tears, and she did not have to
search long for their cause. The picture of Brendan
raising his glass to his beautiful girlfriend, who had raised
hers to him, linking her little finger with his, returned
to haunt her.

There was no doubt in her mind that the day Mrs
Stewart had left she too should have gone, leaving behind
the man with whom she had fallen so desperately, and
so pointlessly, in love. His grandmother had tried to warn
her, had told her of Drusilla's place in his life. She should
have heeded that warning—but when, she asked herself,
had the emotions ever listened to good old common
sense?

Lost in the music, she did not hear the door open and
her heart jumped madly when Brendan thrust his way

into the room. She saw him through the mist of her tears, jerking upright and dashing them away.

As he crossed the room, silencing the music, she pushed the tape recorder under a cushion because explaining its existence there would involve having to tell him her secret.

Glancing at him, she could see that he was angry, and, it seemed, with her. So what was new about that? she asked herself.

He turned sharply. 'The light's on in your bedroom. Why?'

She shrugged, swinging her legs to the floor and easing her straight skirt back over her knees. 'I must have forgotten to turn it off.'

'So Keston's gone.'

'His name,' she corrected him testily, 'is Clive. And for your information he never *came*, so he couldn't *go*, could he? He dropped me outside and didn't receive the invitation he'd hoped for.' She stared up at him. 'Did you think, *really* think I'd taken him up there and——?'

He stood, hands in his trouser pockets, staring down at her, his expression stony.

'What an opinion you must have of my character. Not only having the characteristics of a spy, but the morals of a——' She breathed deeply. 'You know what I mean.'

With his foot, he hooked out the piano stool and sat on it, leaning back against the closed piano lid.

'Do I?' With hooded eyes he looked her over, slowly folding his arms. 'I can't see where morals come into it. Unless you're secretly married? No? Engaged? So there's no one you're letting down? Then where's the low morality in making love with a man?'

She leaned back against the sofa cushions, crossing her legs and spreading her arms. Following the path of his eyes, she saw that her straight skirt had ridden high and that it was her thighs that were in his line of sight.

She uncrossed her legs and made an effort to tug the hem into place, only to discover that her attempt at modesty had brought a twist to his mouth.

'So I've got the green light from you, have I,' she queried, 'to allow Clive Keston into my bed?'

She knew she was provoking him, but at that time of night was beyond caring. What she did not know was how he would react to her pin-pricks. It took about three seconds for her question to be answered.

His jaw thrust forward and his long legs lifted him from the piano seat, taking him across to stand in front of her. He reached down and grasped under her armpits, a roaring fire in his eyes, his lips a straight, menacing line.

The impact of her body against his took the breath from her lungs even as his mouth hit hers, his lips bruising hers as he forced an entry into the moistness he sought. His hands pushed their way beneath her buttoned top, sliding round her back and unfastening the hooks that kept in place the barrier he was determined to storm.

The gasp she gave as his palms slid over her swelling softness was taken into his mouth, her lips opening wider to allow him even greater access. It was only when she felt the air on her skin that she realised her blouse had fallen away, leaving her exposed to his burning gaze from the waist upwards.

'You,' he declared through taut lips, 'will allow no man into your bed except me. Understand?' The shake he gave her forced her back and forward, coming to rest on his shoulder as she moaned with delight under the stroking but none too tender touch of his hands on her breasts. 'Answer me,' he demanded against her lips, 'or I'll——'

'I understand,' she whispered, just before his teeth captured her tongue and her legs sagged beneath her.

When he impelled her down, she hit the sofa seconds in advance of his body coming down on hers.

'Brendan,' she whispered hoarsely, knowing that only a few minutes separated her from total submission to him, 'I—I don't want to lose my job. You—you know what your grandmother said . . . no involvement between us, or else I'd have to go.'

He seemed oblivious to her plea, his tongue drawing pulsating circles around the proud pink tips, arousing her so much that she arched against him. He lifted his head, eyes on fire.

'This time,' he said thickly, 'I'll join you in *your* bed, and this time you . . . will . . . not . . . deny me.'

He lifted himself from her and slid his arms beneath her compliant body. Her arms wound themselves around his neck and she forgot that her job was in jeopardy if she succumbed to his caresses, forgot everything except that she loved him and that it was the most natural thing in the world to make love with the man who meant more to her than any other person on earth . . .

There was a clatter as he swung her round towards the door and his foot caught an object which went flying across the carpet in front of them.

Surprised, he halted, looking down in the subdued lighting of the music-room to catch a glimpse of whatever had fallen to the ground. The tape recorder! Terri guessed at once and the haze in which her senses had been drifting melted away as though it had never been.

It must have slipped from beneath the cushion as Brendan had picked her up. No more than a second passed before he identified it.

Her feet hit the ground and as he bent to pick up the recorder she dived for her clothes, pulling them on even as his gaze seared her bare skin.

No sensuality in his eyes now, only condemnation and censure as he held up the recorder. 'Proof that I've been right not to trust you? Indisputable evidence to support my suspicions?'

Wildly she shook her head. 'I don't know what you're talking about.' Her hands shook as she tried to smooth her hair. She wrested the recorder from his fingers and switched it on, relieved beyond words that she had run it back and erased her futile creative efforts.

'There you are,' she cried, 'nothing, a blank tape.'

'So what does that prove? You must have bought it for some special purpose. Or,' he added with a cynical lift of an eyebrow, 'has my grandmother come into the twentieth century and taken to dictating her business affairs into it?'

'Of course not. I borrowed it from Clive——' She stopped, horrified. Now what would Brendan think?

His lips thinned. 'So the evening out was not just for— shall we say, relaxation? It was business mixed with pleasure.'

'No, it wasn't. It was——'

'Pure pleasure.' His mouth twisted. 'You must tell me his technique some time. Getting you to say yes——'

'I did not say yes. Otherwise, I wouldn't have been sitting here alone listening to music, would I?'

With a smothered imprecation, he swung round and left her.

It was early the following evening before she saw him again. All day, as she'd dealt with her employer's business matters and informed the various friends who had written of Mrs Stewart's absence abroad, her mind had drifted back and forth to the man who had caused her night to be restless and seemingly endless.

Clive had joined her for lunch. 'How are the recording sessions going?' he had asked. 'Is the great work taking shape now? Are the words jumping from your brain on to the tape, for instance?'

Terri had made a face, wishing he wouldn't keep asking her. 'Exactly the opposite. Just looking at the thing dries me up. Would you like it back?' She had taken the recorder from her pocket and offered it to him across the table.

He had shaken his head. 'Keep trying. It's a different technique from writing in longhand, but it'll come, I'm sure it will.'

She'd lifted her shoulders. 'I doubt it, but if you don't want it back yet...' She had returned it to her pocket.

'The search for a secretary—we've drawn a blank,' he'd told her as they'd finished their meal. 'George suggested to Brendan that we should approach you. That is, ask you nicely, but that man Stewart's as stubborn as a mule. Yet he knows as much as we do that we need that empty chair at our talking sessions like we need a hole in the head.'

Terri had returned to Mrs Stewart's office and taken out the tape recorder, staring at it. Tentatively, she had switched it on, taken a breath and started to speak. This time, the sound of her own voice had not proved a barrier to the flow of words that had come from her lips, from deep inside her. She had told herself triumphantly that she was on her way at last!

Now, she watched Brendan's tall, striding figure, his zipped jacket billowing in the evening's strong breeze, moving along the road which led past the house towards the hills. She had, in the past, walked some of its distance with Snippet, and wondered how far Brendan would go.

Darkness was approaching, the line of clouds heralding night moving strategically closer. Without warning, there surfaced inside her a driving need to run after him, catch him up and implore him to listen to her. Anything, she thought, to clear the air between them, to see him smile at her again, to feel his touch... She'd tell him—what would she tell him?

Pulling her jacket from its hanger, she tugged it on,
wound her Stewart tartan scarf around her neck and
slipped into walking shoes. She raced down the stairs,
hauling open the front entrance door, slamming it shut.
Then she pounded along the road, slowing not only for
breath, but to quieten her footsteps so that Brendan
would not know he was being followed.

He branched off the road and began to climb, picking
his way over rocks and boulders and making for a
roughly hewn bench-seat which was perched unexpectedly on one of the rare pieces of flat land.

Slowing to a stop, she held back as he lowered himself
to the seat, spreading his arms along the back and
staring—unseeingly, she was sure—at the view. What,
she wondered, were his thoughts?

She was no more than a few steps away now and, since
she couldn't advance or retreat without his hearing her,
she took a step upwards. He turned, slowly and unsurprised, which indicated, she realised with some embarrassment, that he must have known all along that she
was behind him.

Instead of joining him, she pretended to inspect the
cairn, a cone-shaped pile of stones which had been built
only a few feet past the bench. Words had been en-
graved around the base, but had been so worn by time
and erosion that they were not now decipherable.

'Brendan?' She had meant her voice to ring with confidence, and was annoyed to hear instead the tremulous
note it held.

'Well?'

What had she expected? she reflected unhappily. To
hear him answer, Yes, darling?

'Why won't you trust me?' The long silence was in-
terwoven with the rising whine of the wind. Her jacket
flapped, her hair streamed behind her and she shivered.

'I——' She took a deep breath and heard her inner
voice plead, Don't do it. She fought with her creative

instinct, turned deaf to the playing back in her mind of her sister's cautionary words, and went on, 'I could tell you...' She breathed deeply of the fresh, swirling air. 'I could tell you why I wanted to use that pocket recorder Clive lent me.' She dared not glance at him for fear of seeing the dismissal in his expression.

'And also,' she forced herself to continue, 'why I'm always making notes. And—and looking round doors, and into other people's rooms.' Another pause. 'Do you want to know? Well, even if you don't, I'm going to tell you.'

Her hand reached for the top of the cairn and clung to its ancient solidity. 'I know how much your research team needs secretarial help and I'm willilng to give it, so even if you aren't interested I'm going to clear myself in your eyes, so that you aren't suspicious of me any more.'

She half turned, still not looking at him. 'Please— please note——' she was determined to keep her voice steady '—that this is going to hurt me much more than you. I'm—I'm making notes for a—a——' she just *had* to continue now '—a story my sister has commissioned me to write for her magazine. So, you see, you needn't be suspicious of me any more. And if you're wondering why I haven't told you until now, it's because of Madge's warning.' She blurted out what that warning was.

He still made no move, neither to express belief nor distrust. So, she had to face it; her confession, her efforts to clear herself, had not been accepted.

'Goodnight, Brendan,' she whispered, and picked her steps carefully downwards.

CHAPTER NINE

IN A flash Brendan was on his feet, two strides taking him to Terri's side.

'Oh, no, you don't.' His hand around her wrist pulled her across to sprawl beside him on the bench, and he watched as she straightened herself. 'Now tell me again,' he demanded, listening intently as she repeated her confession almost word for word.

'You swear that this is true? That there's no other explanation for your—I have to say it—furtive interest in the events taking place around you?'

'There's no other explanation. I swear, Brendan, that I've told you the truth.'

'And do I have your permission to verify all you've told me by contacting your sister?'

She had gone so far now that there was no turning back. 'You do. But she's in New York, and so is Leslie, her husband. I had a card from them the other day. They managed to coincide their business affairs so that they could be away together.' She explained their holiday plans, which would keep them away from home for some weeks.

'Will you be able to trust me until they come back?' She smiled up at him. 'In the circumstances, you really haven't any choice, have you?'

'No need for impudence,' he reprimanded her, flicking her cheek.

The setting sun coloured the sky, the hills massed darkly against the brilliant orange and red, the clouds vying with them to add the greatest drama to the brooding evening light.

He tipped her chin up and in the dying remnants of the day looked into her face. 'There's the glow of the sunset in your eyes,' he commented softly.

That glow isn't from the sunset, she wanted to tell him, it comes from inside me, because at last we seem to be at one with each other. Oh, God, she thought, her eyelids fluttering closed, I just hope it stays that way.

His hand fastened around her neck. 'Open your eyes,' he commanded. 'Look at me.'

She saw a tautness about his cheekbones, his gaze half hooded, his hair tossed by the breeze. His purposeful lips descended and she knew she would never, however long she lived, love any man more than she loved Brendan Stewart.

Don't, an inner voice warned. Remember what he said...no commitment...bliss without the wedded. But his kiss blotted out all doubt, all resistance, all thoughts about the future.

When his arms gathered her to him, she went without qualm, without demur. When his fingers slid the zipped jacket opening low enough for his hand to find its way through her layers of clothing to her breasts, she gasped not at his audacity, but at the pleasure of his stroking touch.

He forced her lips wider for greater access and she revelled in the heat he was arousing in her, the desire she had never felt before for a man.

When at last he lifted his head, the dark clouds had won the battle and swallowed the sun whole. 'If,' he growled, 'we were in a kinder landscape——' he gestured to the rocky terrain around them '—I'd take you, Terri Butler, here and now.'

'Take you', he'd said. There was warmth in his tone, anticipation, certainty of physical fulfilment...but where was the love?

'The—the woman in your life wouldn't like it,' she joked hoarsely.

'What woman?' His tone was sharper now.

'Your colleague. Her name's——'

'Leave my *colleague* out of this, will you?'

So he was tacitly admitting, was he, that Drusilla
Jameson, his *colleague*, was the woman in his life?

'Come, Terri.' His hand caught hers and he steadied
her progress down the rock-strewn slope to the road. 'Or
they'll be sending out a search party.'

Don't you mean, she thought but did not say, that
your colleague Drusilla would think the worst and come
and look for you?

Drusilla was in fact wandering around the entrance to
the extension as they made their way towards it. Brendan
had released Terri's hand as they had approached the
house. All the same, Drusilla's jealous eyes must have
picked up the vibrations, the apparent closeness, because her mouth quivered with an internal anger that
seemed to consume her whole body.

'Brendan, darling.'

How she had managed to infuse such tenderness into
her words while her whole body seemed consumed with
animosity Terri did not know.

'A word?' A glance hit Terri like a pebble flung hard.
'Business, darling, purely business. Yes?'

Without hesitation, Brendan strode across to join her.
Had he forgotten that kiss already? And had he, Terri
wondered disconsolately, heard the invitation wrapped
around Drusilla's last word?

The following evening, she sat for a long time at the
small table in her room, notepad open, pencil poised.
Earlier that day she had returned the tape recorder with
thanks to its owner. Closing her eyes, she tried to think
herself back into her story. Even with total concentration, no words would come.

If I were that character, she thought, I'd say... what
would I say? All she could visualise was Brendan's intent

look as his mouth lowered to hers; all she could hear was his voice, husky with desire, saying, 'I'd take you, Terri Butler, here and now...' and, 'Leave my *colleague* out of this...'

Take you, not love you, *take* you, not *love* you... The words went round and round in her head. She threw down the pencil and held her head. So Madge had been right. 'Tell no one or it will go, tell no one...' She had told. It had gone.

Terri put aside the morning's newspaper and answered the phone call.

Without introduction, Brendan asked, 'Would you be free in half an hour to come over and help us out?'

He had opted to sleep sometimes in a room in the extension while his colleagues were in residence. In case, he'd explained to his grandmother who had listened with amusement, inspiration struck any of them in the night and they felt the need to talk.

'You mean,' Terri queried, still not believing her ears, 'that you want me to take Moira's place and——?'

'I do.'

'You're accepting me, just like that?'

'Not exactly. My grandmother gave me the key to her private documents cabinet. I read the contents of your personal file.' A pause. 'I've never doubted that you've got brains. So, how about it?'

'I couldn't refuse the master of the house, could I, even if I wanted to?' she joked. 'Or should I say, as Harvey might, the laird of the hoose?'

He laughed. 'Be careful. That "laird", as you call me, might exercise his rights in other—er—situations. Yes?'

'No.'

He laughed again. 'I had a card from the grand lady in question this morning. They seem to be having a wow of a time. First Montreal, then Ottawa, Niagara Falls, on to Toronto. Lake Ontario's amazing, she says, like an inland sea.'

'I had a card, too,' Terri told him. 'The CN Tower's fantastic, she says, the view from it unbelievable. And now, it seems, they've deviated from their original plan and flown to Vancouver—lovely city, she says. Also, they're about to take a coach tour through the Canadian Rockies and back.'

'They certainly do seem to be getting around. So— thirty minutes?'

She dealt with her employer's affairs in ten.

'Hi, Terri,' came from all directions when she entered the meeting-room.

'Are we pleased to see you!' said George Smythe, grey-haired, benign and very learned-looking. 'Our wrists have almost been falling off with writing the minutes of our meetings.'

Drusilla, seated beside Clive, was the only person at the oval-shaped table who failed to greet her. Her pale eyes did not miss Brendan's pointing finger indicating to Terri that she should take the seat beside him.

'I trust that Miss Butler has received sufficient education,' she commented in a falsely bored tone, 'to enable her at least to spell correctly the scientific terms that we use?'

'Claws in, Drusilla,' one of the men said under his breath.

'Miss Butler has certificates in three science subjects,' Brendan informed her, his voice conveying the message, Matter closed.

'Terri?' Clive held out his pocket recorder. 'Yes?'

She felt rather than saw the tension in Brendan's demeanour as his gaze slewed round to see the nature of the object that Clive was passing her down the table.

'You mean for helping with the note-taking? Well, yes, thanks.' She reached across the table to take it. 'That is,' she asked Brendan, 'if you have no objection?'

The shoulder beside her shrugged. 'If that's what you want. If it helps you.'

'Makes for greater accuracy,' the young man she knew to be Bill Parton pointed out.

Terri nodded. 'I'll take notes to back it up.'

'Good.' Brendan slanted a glance down at her. 'All set?' His smile turned her heart over.

As she listened to the proceedings, recording them and writing simultaneously, Terri was astonished at how argumentative the members of the team seemed to be. Did they ever agree on anything? she wondered. On almost every subject there seemed to be objections to every angle put forward as a basis for the project's progress.

She noted, looking up now and then, how often Clive leaned towards Drusilla, whispering in her ear. How often, too, Drusilla shook her head, or pointed with a stabbing motion at her notes or his.

To Terri's surprise, Brendan let it pass, although she was sure he was aware of what was going on.

'The trials; how are they progressing?' enquired Barry Henderson.

'No reliable results yet, apparently,' Clive told him.

'What we have got is encouraging,' Drusilla put in, ignoring the implied threat in Clive's fist thrust, with apparent playfulness, at her chin.

As the group dispersed and Brendan became engaged in conversation with some of the others, Clive approached.

'You look bewildered,' he commented.

'I didn't realise how quarrelsome scientists could be. I thought Brendan did a great job in the chair.'

'Keeping his rowdy colleagues in order? Yeah. He's standing right behind you,' Clive warned.

Turning, Terri met Brendan's eyes. Something seemed to spark between them.

'I guess I've had a lot of practice,' was Brendan's drawling comment. He turned back to his colleagues and moved away with them.

'Don't do it,' came Clive's murmured warning.

'Do what?'

'Fall for the guy. He's practised in the art of seduction. Anyway, he's not for you. You'd want permanency, wouldn't you?'

'How do you know?'

'You're transparent. In that respect, at least. Anyway, his sensual reflexes, to put it politely, have found another outlet. You get me?'

The gaze she turned upon him was, she hoped, unreadable.

'So take my advice, chick.' She bridled inwardly at the word. 'You don't want to get hurt, do you? Now, I——' he crooked his arm '——I'd be prepared to make a commitment. With the right woman. So how about——?'

Terri looked at his arm. The invitation it held did nothing to her. She looked up. 'Sorry. But thanks anyway.'

A shadow passed across his gaze and for some inexplicable reason Terri felt a shiver course through her.

'Thanks for the words of wisdom, though.'

Christiana Stewart telephoned in the late afternoon. After the usual enquiries as to the health and well-being of her grandson and her secretary, she asked how that secretary was occupying her time.

'That young man's taken my advice, has he? I should think so too. I hoped he would answer. I told him exactly the time of my call. Here in Vancouver we are eight hours behind you. Why is he not there to talk to me?'

A sound behind her had Terri swinging round. 'Here he is now, Mrs Stewart.'

Brendan glanced at his watch, turning down the corners of his mouth. 'Sweet or sour?' he mouthed.

'In between.' As she handed over the receiver, their fingers touched. His glance at her had nothing whatever to do with the telephone call and her heart turned over.

'Hi, Grandmother.' He turned away. 'Yes, I'm OK. Tell me about you. Are you and Annie having a great time? You're hoping to see some bears on your Rockies tour? Don't count on it. And if you do see any, don't call them "teddy" and try to hug them, will you? They're dangerous creatures.' He smiled at the reprimand that Terri guessed must have come his way.

'Am I maintaining my hands-off policy towards your secretary? First of all, and with respect, it's not *my* policy, Grandmother, it's yours. And second, she's my secretary now, too. OK,' he said more seriously, and with a faint note of irritation, 'I hear what you say.'

He talked on and Terri busied herself with the notes she had taken, uncovering the typewriter and rolling in a sheet of paper.

Call over, Brendan approached the desk. 'Whose work are you about to do?'

'You mean, your grandmother's or yours? Some of each.'

'I'd prefer you to use the office in the extension for the group's affairs. You can use Moira's desk. There's a word processor there. Better than this steam-age contraption.' His hand dismissed the small, somewhat ancient portable machine on which she typed her employer's letters.

'Where Moira used to work?' She lifted her shoulders. 'If you wish.'

'I wish.'

The tone had her head lifting sharply. The brooding look in his eyes made her heart miss a beat.

'The *hands-on* approach makes for better business relationships. Yes?'

She knew what he meant, and it had nothing to do with business. Say yes, her heart answered. No, never, her common sense argued.

'You——' She moistened her lips, strangely dry. 'You heard your grandmother's warning. And anyway, I don't want to lose my job.' His hand came out. She backed away. 'Brendan...' If he so much as touched her, she was lost.

He thrust his hands into his pockets. His whole demeanour... his dark eyes with a storm brewing in them, the deep intelligence in his face—all combined to form a magnet so powerful that she had to reinforce all her defences to resist the pull of him.

'Don't back away from me.' Spoken slowly, the statement held a faint menace. He swung round, halted at the door. 'I'm going over to the cottage. Will you come, please?' No overtones of things sensual now, but a businesslike demand. 'My papers over there are in a mess. I'd like your help with sorting through them.' He seemed to take her agreement for granted. 'Get a jacket.' Then softly came the words, 'Not mine.'

He was remembering the jacket she'd borrowed from him! So she would let him know that she, too, remembered.

Head on one side, she asked, 'Are we rowing across?'

His gaze flickered. She had touched his 'replay' button. 'No, we are not,' he said firmly, as if to a truculent child. 'Car.'

Fetching her jacket, she swung it on. The road curved back on itself, taking them round the inlet. The memories his cottage brought back almost hurt in their intensity. Braking outside, he waited. Wondering why, she turned her head and caught his hooded expression, tuning in to his thoughts, to *his* memories. Her pulse-rate accelerated, warmth crept into her cheeks.

'You want help?' she prompted. 'With your *business* affairs?'

He smiled and her heart spun. 'I note the emphasis. That's me put in my place. OK.' He heaved his tough frame out of the car. 'Business it is.'

They worked until dusk came. Terri sighed, sitting back on her heels at the base of the filing cabinet. They were in the room, the unlocked room, which had so intrigued her when she had stayed the night there, years ago, it seemed to her now.

'Where chaos reigned, tidiness now prevails, to coin a phrase,' she stated with satisfaction. She looked over the length of him, noting the well-fitting cord trousers, the loose dark sweater over an open-necked shirt, and felt the customary pull of him. 'How long will it last?'

'For as long as you're around to wave your magic wand.'

She shook her head. 'I didn't achieve it alone. You co-operated.'

There was a long pause, then, 'Would you co-operate?'

Her short, sharp sigh was meant to convey aggravation. He would never know that each time he issued his veiled invitation it became more difficult to say no.

She stood up, going to the typewriter. 'Shall I sign off here?'

'Yes, do that,' he called over his shoulder. 'I'll make us some tea.'

Terri stood looking down at the closed-in stove, now cold, and recalled the night Snippet had basked in its warmth on the hearthrug... Would she, she wondered, if the situation ever arose again of needing to share Brendan's bed, would she let him...?

'Tea.' Startled out of the past, she jumped. 'Where were you?' Brendan asked. His smile was just a little goading. 'If you were where I thought you were, I'm game. Just say the word.'

She turned on him. '*Will* you drop the subject? Will you stop provoking me?'

'It's called wearing you down.' He had spoken so un-emotionally, she felt her anger leave her. He handed her some tea, offered her an opened packet of biscuits. Feeling just a little foolish over her outburst, she took one, wandering to the window.

The landscape was darkening, the surrounding hills having almost disappeared. The waves washed the shoreline, rocking the moored rowing boat. It had been on this side, after all. At some time, Brendan must have rowed it back.

'Your sister's still away.'

'Yes.' Stiffening, she addressed his reflection in the uncurtained window. 'How did you know?'

'I phoned her office. Her deputy told me. She confirmed that she and her husband have gone on a working holiday in the States.'

She drank some tea, returning the mug to the table and dusting her hands free of biscuit crumbs. He watched her over the rim of his mug, swallowing some liquid, as if assessing her reaction to his words.

'May I ask why you called my sister's office?' Her voice was thin, instead of ringing with indignation as she had intended. 'No, let me guess. To check on me.'

'Right.'

'So you didn't believe me after all when I told you I was gathering the ideas for a story?'

'The deputy editor said she had heard nothing about it.'

'It was between my sister and myself. I wish I'd never told you.' Did her voice have to waver? She turned away. 'My sister would have confirmed what I told you.' To her horror, her voice was thick. 'So get another secretary. I don't care.' But she did; it showed in her voice, the way her wrists tried to stem the tears.

'Terri.' Her name was a whisper on his lips, his hands, as he stood behind her, moving from her shoulders, over her waist to rest there. 'Turn around.' She did not move and his fingers, moving to her hips, eased her round to face him.

The feel of his hands on her body made her hold her breath. If he pulled her to him now...

One hand went to his trouser pocket and he drew something from it. It was a bunch of keys and he slipped his finger into the keyring so that they jangled.

She could only stare.

'For you. For this place. A duplicate set. You don't believe me?' He took her hand, palm upwards, and dropped the keys into it, closing her fingers over them. 'I trust you that much.' He tipped her chin, rubbing at the tears with his thumb. 'Now what do you say?'

'Thanks,' was all she could manage, slipping the keys into her trouser pocket.

'And?' It was a whisper.

She looked into his eyes and was lost. Only on tiptoe could she fulfil his expectation, placing her mouth softly against his.

'You can do better than that,' he growled, and took her in his arms, bending back her head under the pressure of his kiss. His hands were not idle, finding her hips again and massaging the flesh against the bone, slipping round to her rear and jerking her against his unmistakable arousal.

'I want you,' came from him thickly. 'Right now. And you want me; don't try to deny it.

Somehow she summoned the strength to escape his hold, hurting herself in the process. But that was better, wasn't it, she asked herself fiercely, than the deep emotional—and probably never-ending—hurt she would suffer if she let him have his way?

'I—I may sound old-fashioned——' how she managed the sarcasm she would never know '—but I like a little love mixed in with the lust. And from *you* I know I wouldn't get it.'

His jaw jutted, his eyes half closed. 'So experienced she sounds, when there I was thinking how fresh and unviolated the lady was. So who's offered you the *love* you crave? Clive Keston?'

Clive had, in a fashion, although she wasn't going to tell this man. Nevertheless, he guessed. 'So Keston's got that far under your defences, has he? You know his reputation?'

'No, but I know yours,' was torn from her.

'He's a silky, smooth-talking bastard. If he's passed first base with you, you can go to——'

'I'm not taking your insults another minute.' Seizing her jacket from a chair, she pulled it on, running out on to the dark road, following the shoreline, and keeping on running, although unable to see more than a few steps ahead of her.

A car started up, drawing level. She went on running. A few thudding strides later, she was struggling in powerful arms as from behind they bundled her into the passenger seat.

He drove fast, saying nothing. She withdrew the keys and banged them on to the dashboard. 'I don't want them.'

He let the action pass, bringing the car to a stop in front of the house. He picked up the keys and slid them back into her pocket, his hand lingering there familiarly.

'Love,' he grated, 'may be great while it lasts. But when it's snatched from you, it's like a dagger sinking in. It half kills you. But in my book that doesn't exclude *making* it.'

His mouth touched her throat and it was almost her undoing, but he let her go and she managed to reach her room before she allowed the tearing, racking sobs to have their way.

CHAPTER TEN

'WE SHOULD publish, I tell you,' Clive, voice raised, was saying.

'We will not publish. Not until we're good and ready. You get me?' Brendan's voice was quiet but deadly in its insistence and authority.

'OK,' Clive retorted, 'so our rivals will get in there first and get all the honour and register the patent. Not to mention receive the prize money.'

Terri heard the argument as she entered the office in the extension two mornings later. The voices came from the meeting-room next door.

'OK, I know what you're going to say next,' Brendan put in crisply. 'That that money will go towards their future research, which will take them even further ahead of us. So what? We're working for a cure, not kudos, not cash prizes.'

'You're too bloody good to be true,' Clive returned. 'It's a big, cruel world out there——'

'And lay off Terri Butler.'

Terri's heart jumped, staring at the communicating door. The unexpected change of subject silenced Clive, but only for a moment.

'She's *your* property, is she?' came his sneering reply. 'Well, a word of advice, pal. Guard your freedom. She's out for permanence, no less.'

The door flung itself open under Terri's hand and she hurled herself into the room. 'Stop talking about me, do you hear? You're a miserable lot, both of you. I wouldn't touch either of you——' her eyes swung from

Clive's to Brendan's, where they faltered and fell '—if you were offered to me with a fortune attached.'

She swung the door hard behind her, leaving behind a deathly silence. Then a door banged and someone went away. The connecting door opened and Terri became aware of Brendan standing there.

She lifted her head from the papers she was pretending to study. 'Thank you for trying to protect my virtue,' she said, head high, 'but I don't need you, or any man, to defend something that is my concern entirely.'

'As if I didn't know,' he said.

'Know what?'

'That permanence in a relationship is your highest priority.'

'Which is why we go together like—like milk and vinegar. We turn each other off.'

On the desk the phone rang. Terri listened, and looked at Brendan. 'Yes, Miss Jameson, Dr Stewart is here. Right.' She put the phone down. 'Your lady friend calls, Dr Stewart. Why——' did her voice have to tremble? '—don't you go to her? She'll give you what you want. She's far more familiar with your—your requirements than I am.'

He did not move, except that his expression had hardened.

'I'm sorry,' she said, closing her eyes. 'While I'm working for you, I have no right to talk to you like that.'

He nodded, accepting her apology, but there was ice in his eyes as the door closed between them.

Using the keys that Brendan had given her, Terri let herself into the cottage.

As she had left the house across the inlet, she had taken a phone call from her employer. Terri had explained that Brendan had gone south for a week, but was expected back any time.

'How are you getting on?' she'd asked.

'I enjoyed every moment of our Rockies tour,' Mrs Stewart had answered. 'Wonderful scenery, excellent hotels. Now we're back in Vancouver and I've fallen hard for the place. Annie and I plan to take the ferry across to Vancouver Island and stay for a few days in Victoria. After that, we'll discuss our next destination.' A short silence had followed, then, 'If only I didn't feel so tired.'

Alarm bells had rung in Terri's head. 'You're doing too much, Mrs Stewart,' she'd declared anxiously. 'Can't you slow down a bit?'

'Over on the island, we'll take it easy, dear, don't worry. Otherwise, we're fine, both of us.'

Opening the door into the cottage, Terri made for Brendan's office. Having had permission from Mrs Stewart to use the car whenever she wanted, she had driven round the inlet along the narrow road and parked on a rock-roughened area to the right of the white-washed building.

On a sheet of paper in large letters on the desk was a note:

Please distribute the following memo to each member of the team: The project may be nearing a successful conclusion, but *we will not publish yet*. Too bad if our rivals get there first. I would sooner *they* made a hash of things than for us to rush in before the trials are complete. Signed, Brendan C. Stewart.

There was a movement behind her. Stifling a gasp, she swung round. It was not the owner who stood there, nor even a stranger, but Clive Keston. The familiar feeling of anxiety arose in her at the sight of him, although she told herself she had no reason whatever to be concerned about his motives. After all, he was Leslie's friend, wasn't he?

'Hi there.'

'Did you come by car?' Terri had her answer as she looked out of the window and saw his car parked behind hers outside. 'I didn't hear you arrive.'

'Nor should you have. That vehicle cost a small fortune.'

Before she could take action, he was looking over her shoulder at the memo. 'So I get to read his lordship's— or should I say lairdship's?—directive first. He won't budge?' He turned a smile on Terri but it was, she noticed, tarnished at the edges. 'How is it——' he stared around '—that you've been granted the honour of the freedom of his hideaway? There's this rumour circulating that there's something big between you.'

If only there were, she thought. 'Not even something small,' she answered.

'Maybe he's here?'

Terri shook her head. 'You should know that he's away.'

'Oh, yes,' he said with a testing side-glance, 'with the lady in his life.'

This she hadn't known. Her spirits sank, but she kept her expression carefully blank. The phone rang.

'You've got company in my cottage?' Brendan's words grazed Terri's ear. Even so, her heart leapt at hearing his voice after seven of the longest days of her life.

'As a matter of fact, I have.' She kept her tone light. 'Clive's here. Which you no doubt knew anyway, with the help of your binoculars.' This was better, she thought; attack, don't defend.

'You don't need optical assistance when the sight of *two* cars tells you all you need to know. Spoilt your assignation, did I, by returning unexpectedly?'

'If you think that,' she blurted out, unnerved by the ferocity of his tone, 'then you'll think *anything* of me.'

She flung down the receiver, meeting Clive's wide gaze. 'If you talk to Himself in that tone,' he said, 'then you just have to be on familiar terms with the guy.'

'For God's sake.' She sank into the office chair. 'First *you* set me up as *his* lover, then *he* as good as accuses me of having an affair with *you*.'

'Any time, Terri, any time.' He crooked his arm. With a smile, she shook her head and he shrugged, minus a reciprocal smile.

The phone rang again. 'I want Clive over here. And you, too, if you can tear yourselves away from each other.'

'You heard?' Terri queried, replacing the receiver.

'Yep. Bad mood.' He moved to the door. 'That's interesting. The result, maybe, of his snooping activities down south? That's why he went, didn't you know?'

'Snooping into what?' But Clive was making for his car, and drove away with a wave.

'I'm happy to tell you,' Brendan addressed his eager-eyed colleagues seated around the large rectangular table, 'that, as a result of my enquiries during my week's stay in the south, I've discovered that our rivals are some way behind us in their research.' Silent claps and muted hoorays greeted his words. 'Therefore, we can stop worrying about staking our claim to everlasting fame too soon——' here there were sniggers '—and registering our own progress by rushing into print.'

Clive and one or two others shook their heads. Drusilla, dressed in tight blue trousers and matching long, belted tunic, doodled on her notepad. She had just returned, Terri reminded herself with grudging admiration, from a long and tiring car journey, yet this had not detracted one bit from her feminine attractions.

Pushing at her own hair, she wished she'd had the foresight to guess that Brendan might return that day and had taken more care with her own appearance.

'So,' commented Brendan, one arm over the back of his upright chair, 'I put it to the meeting that a celebration wouldn't be out of place.'

The suggestion was passed unanimously and Bill and Barry offered to help with the arrangements. They filed out, laughing and talking, Drusilla in deep conversation with Clive.

Terri made to follow, but remembered the call from Canada. 'Your grandmother's enjoying every minute,' she told him, telling him also of the two ladies' plans. He nodded, hands in pockets. 'Something she said worried me.' He frowned, waiting for more. 'She was tired, she said. I told her to slow down, take it easy for a while.'

'Good advice. I'm sorry I wasn't here. I'd have told her to come home. Not that she would have listened.' He walked halfway round the table, walked back. 'What is it between you and Keston?'

Terri's skin prickled. 'What could there be? I suppose you're asking why he was over there,' dipping her head in the direction of the cottage. 'The answer is, I don't know. He must have known I was there because of the car.'

'Which is the answer you're looking for.'

'Look, Brendan, there's nothing between us. He's— he's not my type.'

'No? But I guess you're his. However, for once I wasn't referring to romantic intrigue.'

She shook her head, bewildered. 'What were you referring to, then?'

He straightened from the door against which he had been leaning. 'OK, forget it.'

She made for the door, but needed to pass him, tensing against the pull of him.

'Terri.'

It was neither a question nor a statement and her heart, already beating fast, went into training for the Olympics. His eyes busied themselves all over her and it was as if they were doing a memory check of all her features.

She drew a breath and told herself to stop imagining the impossible. 'Yes, Dr Stewart?' As an attempt to normalise the situation, it fell by the wayside.

'How long did seven days seem to you?'

Should she tell him? Her lips made their own decision. 'S-seven weeks, Dr Stewart.' Her eyes met his and again she found herself speaking. 'What about you?'

'Seven years.'

Somehow the distance between them disappeared and she was in his arms, her notebook and pencil hitting the floor.

'Oh, Brendan, I——' was all she managed before his mouth took hers, invading and plundering and robbing her lungs of breath. When he finally let her go, her forehead found his chest, while her arms wrapped themselves around his neck, her fingers even taking it upon themselves to run through his hair.

It hurt, this pleasure she felt at being one with him again, a delight and a pain, because her reason kept nagging her, He took Drusilla with him when he went south. It's variety this man is seeking, not love, she reminded herself painfully. Wasn't that the message he left you with just before he left?

'My God!' Unheard, the door had burst open and one of the men stood there. Barry, Terri thought. 'At it again, man?'

Brendan swung round without releasing his hold.

'You go off with a woman,' Barry chuckled, 'and come back to a woman. A different one, of course. Wait until Drusilla hears of this.'

'Get out, will you?' Brendan commanded, eyes blazing.

Breaking free, Terri bent to retrieve her notebook and pencil.

'Hey,' Barry commented, glancing over his shoulder, 'talk of the devil. What's the feminine of "devil", Drusilla?'

'"Bitch,"' Drusilla enunciated clearly, her gaze poisonous as it rested on Terri.

'No, wrong species,' Barry declared, still chuckling as he walked away.

Drusilla occupied the doorway. 'Don't take him seriously, Miss Butler, will you? It's his technique for keeping secretaries sweet. In the absence of anyone else, he's making sure you stay.'

'It's OK, Miss Jameson,' Terri responded, keeping a tight control on her hands, which were showing a disconcerting tendency to tremble. 'I never take any of my employer's grandson's amorous advances seriously.'

With which, head high, she swept out.

Entering by the front door, Terri sensed that the atmosphere had somehow changed. Her heart missed a beat. An intruder? Wondering whether to advance or retreat, she left the door open—and was nearly frightened out of her wits when a small bundle of fur swerved around the corner from the kitchen area and, barking its head off, flung itself at her feet.

'Snippet!' she cried, unable to believe her eyes. Bending down, she stroked the wiry body and laughed at the animal's breathless delight.

'Aye, he's pleased to be here again,' said Harvey, drying his hands, an apron tied around his waist and neck. 'And I have tae admit, so am I.'

Terri rose. 'You should have let us know, Harvey,' she said. 'We'd have gone to meet you at the station.'

'I took a taxi. The dog was tired from his journey.'

'I bet you were, too. It's good to have you back,' Terri told him, meaning it.

He inclined his head in thanks and added, 'His lady owner telephoned me at my brother's house. The dog couldn't settle, she said. He must be missing someone, or something.'

Terri nodded. 'The Scottish air, probably, the lovely countryside.'

'Och aye. Anyway, she'd taken on a little job, she said, and thought it wouldn't be fair to the animal to leave him alone in the house for hours. So would I be a dearie and bring him back with me? So here he is.'

Terri started to climb the stairs, laughing as Snippet scampered past her.

'Do you think Mrs Stewart will mind having him back?' Terri asked.

'Not a bit, lassie. Can ye tell me who'll be here for the evening meal? You? And Mr Brendan?'

'Oh.' Sharing a table with Brendan again, having to make polite conversation, when all she really wanted was the language of love...? Snap out of it, she reproached herself. Love—and Brendan Stewart? You must be joking! 'You'd better ask him, Harvey. He's been eating with his colleagues lately, so I doubt if he'll be here. But please don't bother to cook just for me...'

The hurt look on his face made her pause. 'Although,' she added with a smile, 'I'd love to taste your cooking again.'

His good humour restored, Harvey nodded and returned to his domain.

Snippet followed her into her room and sat panting on his haunches. She lifted him on to her lap and hugged his small figure, stroking his fur and trying to blot out of her memory Barry's words: 'At it again, man? You go off with a woman and come back to a woman. Wait until Drusilla...'

And Drusilla's warning, intended to hurt, but probably true: It was Brendan's technique, she'd said, for keeping secretaries happy in their work.

Then her memory played her false, tormenting her by running backwards to those magic moments she had spent in Brendan's arms, his kisses, his words... and the lie implicit in them that he had missed her, seven days for him having equalled seven years...

The slow tears dropped on to the dog's paws, making him jump. He licked them but did not like the taste, jumping from her lap and standing by the door, tail wagging expectantly.

'I get the message,' Terri told him, managing a smile and pulling on a jacket. Downstairs, Snippet leapt at his lead, which hung on its usual hook. 'He can't wait,' she told a smiling Harvey, 'to find his favourite haunts again.'

'Aye, and his favourite trees,' he added, at which Terri laughed, lifting down the lead and pushing it into her pocket.

She had not gone more than a few steps when Snippet's head came up, listening. Barking crazily, he made a mad dash around the corner.

'Hey, who's this little fella?' came a voice so familiar that the tears nearly sprang again. 'What the hell are you doing here? I thought you'd been returned to your owner.' Brendan rounded the corner and halted, the dog leaping at his legs. 'Down, hound.'

It all came back—their first meeting, Snippet's recognition of Brendan's scent on his clothes, the part he'd played in causing Brendan to share the bed—his bed—with her, in the cottage. Snippet dashed off in all directions.

'Harvey's back,' Terri said. Winding the dog's lead round her hand, she explained how it was that Harvey had brought Snippet back with him. Calling to the dog, she made for the road.

'How many copies of the memo did you manage to type out,' Brendan's voice stopped her progress, 'before Keston joined you at the cottage?'

Clenching her teeth, she answered, 'He didn't *join* me. And none, is the answer to your question.'

'You were too busy doing——'

'Yes, I've missed you,' she seethed, glaring at him, 'missed your sarcasm and your cynicism and your innuendoes. And, as they say, what a "good miss" it was.'

'Thanks a lot,' came drily from him. 'I'm going to the cottage now. I'd be obliged if you'd join me there and continue where you left off.'

'But I——' She gestured towards the dog.

'He can come too. He knows the place as well as you do.'

Joyously Snippet bounced into Brendan's car, and with equal pleasure nosed his way into the interior of the cottage, familiarising himself again with the dark corners and the hearthrug, recognising his own scent and curling up there.

As Terri worked, she heard the generator start up. Brendan reappeared and prowled, hands in pockets, deep in thought. Once or twice he used the phone, talking so quietly that Terri could not hear his voice over the clatter of the typewriter. She was overwhelmingly aware of him, her skin prickling as he passed to and fro, her eyes closing as he paused now and then behind her.

It was only when her inner emptiness registered, telling her it was time for food, that she glanced at her watch and saw with a shock how late it was. She went looking for Brendan and found him with Snippet on his lap, absently fondling the dog's ears.

Snippet leapt to the floor and went nosing round the door.

'No walk,' Brendan told him, 'but if you want to go out...' Gladly the dog went, leaving them alone.

'I forgot the time,' Terri said apologetically. 'We should be getting back.'

'Why? There's enough food here to feed an army, including the dog.' At which Snippet, on cue, barked at the closed door, scampering in when it was opened.

'But I told Harvey I'd be in for the evening meal. He'll have cooked——'

'He won't. I called him just after we arrived, telling him thanks, but we'd eat over here.'

'But——' she began, then nodded. Don't, she told herself, argue with the man who is currently employing you. And anyway, the idea of sharing a meal with Brendan over a roughened kitchen table, instead of having to make strained conversation in a stately dining-room, was almost too good to be true.

As it happened, they did not sit at a table, instead eating hunks of bread and cheese and drinking coffee from mugs while seated at—or in Brendan's case on— the desk while he dictated letters and notes arising from his recent absence in the south of the country.

Terri finished her work and told Brendan she had done so, at which he passed her another pile. Yawning, eyes watering with tears of tiredness, she worked on. Pulling a letter from the typewriter, she watched abstractedly as her arm placed itself on a pile of folders on her desk, her head deciding to rest itself there. Only for a moment, she thought, to ease some of the tension from her neck...

In her dream arms gathered her, carrying her through the air, wafting her on a cloud towards the moon. The breeze—or was it a hand?—stroked her hair. The moon went out, just like a light switching off, and the ensuing darkness swallowed her whole.

She woke hours later to find herself in a bed, her legs bare—had *she* removed her trousers?—and alone— wasn't she? No. Someone was there, a muscled human form holding her against him, hard-boned and solid, nothing ethereal or dream-like about him... *Him*?

She tensed, half fearful, half ecstatic. She knew his identity immediately by his own personal scent. In stirring, she had told him of her wakefulness and his lips moved around her ear, his hands turning her towards him. His fingers unfastened buttons, sliding beneath her blouse, skimming over her breasts, slipping under her briefs and across her stomach, making her clench her muscles against the desire that took shocking, wonderful hold of her.

'Brendan, you can't, you mustn't.' Her hands, even as she pleaded with him to stop, clung to his shoulders, his arms. 'My job—I'll lose it. Your grandmother said so.'

'To hell with your job,' he said thickly, his lips and tongue forcing her breasts to give themselves entirely over to his caresses. 'And *we* can, *we* must.'

'But——' How could she tell him that in letting him have his way he would alter her life, because no man would ever mean so much to her again? Which meant— her thoughts were feverish now—that she'd have to live the rest of her life alone, because he would take her and leave her, as he had vowed to do to every woman who came into his life.

'Will you come to me?' Not a question, a demand. 'Seven days equalled seven years, I told you. You were in my dreams, you tortured my sleep. You kept slipping away. Now you're here, beside me, responding—oh, God, how you're responding!'

All of her now was crying out for him, her pulses throbbing, the blood rushing around her heated body.

'What if, Brendan,' she whispered hoarsely, arching against him as he moved over her, 'what if——?'

'I'll take care of that,' came in a murmur from his lips, on a lingering journey from her stomach down and down again...

She gasped out loud when she felt him enter her, heard a small cry come from her throat, moaned when he momentarily held back, then gasped again at the pleasure he began to give her, gently at first, then quickening, carrying her with him until stars exploded in her head and his kiss took over her mouth entirely, holding it as the glow bound them in a bonding so close, she felt she was actually part of him and he of her.

The night receded and he made love to her again. Attuned to him totally now, she held nothing back, giving and taking, until again, as the sun rose, adding its own golden glow, they lay together at last as one.

I love you, I love you. How, she wondered in anguish, could she keep those words from ever being uttered? Because he just wouldn't want to know, would he? It would embarrass him and make him walk away...

He whispered softly in her ear, stroking her throbbing body, chiding her for not telling him.

'You gave me no chance,' she answered, eyes brilliant, dazzled by the brightness in his. 'Knowing I'd never... Would it have stopped you?'

'You know the answer to that,' he replied, starting to caress her all over again.

'It's late,' she said, twisting away and swinging from the bed. 'Beat you to the bathroom.' Aware, with a quick shock, of her nakedness, she seized the first thing she saw—his jacket, pulling it on and turning shy as his eyes raked the part of her that the jacket did not cover.

He dived to get her and held her wrists wide so that the jacket fell open. He caressed her shape with his eyes, then leaned forward, using his lips and tongue to arouse her until her head hung back and she gasped at the erotic pleasure he was giving her.

He started to push the jacket from her shoulders, but she twisted free and reached the bathroom. He pushed against the door and his strength, being greater than hers, succeeded in opening it—when the telephone shrilled harshly in the bedroom.

Smothering a curse, he went to answer it and Terri turned the key, expecting any moment that he would return, hammering on the door and demanding entry.

He did not come and she finished her toilet undisturbed. He must have pulled on some clothes, she decided, and taken Snippet for a walk.

Emerging flushed, bright-eyed and dressed, she discovered that Brendan had not left the cottage. A towel had been twisted across his hips and she laughed at his back as he stared through the bedroom window. 'I beat you to it. Your turn now,' she said.

Still he did not turn so she ran across the bedroom, lifting her hands to his shoulders to make him face her. When he did, she wished she hadn't tried. His face was a mask, eyes ice-cold.

Her heart sank, her lungs would hardly function.

'What's wrong?' She wrapped her arms around her as if to keep out the chill of his eyes. 'Was it that phone call? Has something happened?'

He folded his arms across his chest, that chest over which she had spread tiny kisses, through whose mat of hair she had scratched with her fingernails, then rubbed her cheek—only minutes . . . no, centuries ago!

'You lied to me.'

She caught her breath. 'In—in which respect? You—you know—you discovered for yourself—that you were the first——'

'There is no story,' he broke in, 'that your sister commissioned you to write. What you told me was all *fiction*——' he plainly did not like the word '—even if your *notes* were not. And——' he approached her slowly, jaw set, mouth a straight line '—don't try to deny it. That phone call——'

'Yes?' She frowned. For the life of her she could not think what the call could have been about that would have caused this disastrous alteration of his mood, this change from passionate lover to prosecutor and frightening accuser.

'I have it from none other than your sister that no such commission existed for you to write a story for her magazine.'

'You've spoken to my sister?' Terri whispered. 'But how? She and Leslie are travelling in the States and not even I have been given a phone number which would reach them.'

'I didn't speak directly to her.' He adjusted the towel so that it hung more securely around his waist. 'When I was in London I called her magazine yet again to try to verify your claim of writing for it. As before, I spoke to her deputy, name of Audrey Green. Yes?' Miserably, Terri nodded. 'She told me she managed by sheer luck to catch your sister and her husband in a hotel before they left for their next destination. Which is when your sister denied every claim you've made, asking her to pass this on to me. She said that she would never have given such a commission to anyone but a professional writer, which you are not, and that you must have made the whole thing up, because writing magazine stories has been one of your fantasies from childhood onwards.'

Terri sank on to the bed, shaking her head. 'How——?' She had to clear her throat. 'How *could* she?'

Tears were not far away, of shock, of reaction, of this confirmation, by Brendan's cold and distant manner, that he'd meant every word he had said about enjoying lust without love.

'So——' she lifted her head '—what are you trying to say?' He stayed silent and the answer came to her from nowhere. 'Once you came very near to accusing me of being a spy. Is that what you're now saying bluntly and without sparing my feelings as you did last time? That what I'm really doing here is working for your rivals and trying to discover the chemical formula of the drug you're all researching, so that they can beat you to it and publish first and take out a patent and claim all the honours?'

'You seem to be familiar with the jargon,' he said icily, 'not to mention the procedure.'

'I'm not exactly dumb,' she threw back, 'as——' a sob escaped her control '—as you said soon after I'd met you. Why,' she challenged, 'if you suspected me, did you allow me to sit in on the group's discussions and act as your secretary after Moira left?'

'As I told you when I gave you a set of keys to this place, I trusted you. In the absence, that is, of any evidence to the contrary. Being a scientist, I keep emotion out of my assessment of people. I'd looked up your career details in my grandmother's private file. I could see by looking at your books that you had some knowledge of subjects with a scientific bias.'

'Wasn't it——' she had to hit back and hit hard '—poor judgement on your part to allow someone you suspected even a little bit of having connections with your rivals access to all those notes?'

'No.' He leaned against a cupboard. 'Because I never allowed you within sight of the really important data, the details of the actual formulation of the drug. Nor did I let you see anything connected with the results of the trials, which even now are an ongoing thing.'

She closed her eyes. Checkmate, she thought. Getting to her feet, she stilled the tremble in her lower lip.

'So, I pack my bags and leave. Is that what you're saying?' She was glad that he could not see how her heart was slowly breaking.

A sharp bark made her jump, reminding her of Snippet's presence.

'He wants out,' she said, head high. 'So do I, from—from all this, from *you*.' Reaching into her trouser pocket, she withdrew the set of keys he had given her and tossed them on to the bed.

Swift footsteps took her to the door. 'Thank you,' she said bravely, turning, 'for initiating me into the—the delights of lovemaking. Like—like you...' her throat burned as she forced herself to lie again '...I think *lust* has a lot going for it, without the awful threat of p-permanency hanging over it. I——' Did she have to lynch herself like this? 'I feel I'd like to try it with other men now I know h-how.'

'Why, you——' He made a sharp movement towards her, but checked himself—not, it seemed, without difficulty.

She ran through into the living-room, swept up her jacket and Snippet's lead and, with tears streaming down her cheeks, ran from the cottage with Snippet racing madly ahead.

CHAPTER ELEVEN

How *could* Madge have done it? Terri wondered next morning, staring down at the inlet from the rocky hill she had climbed. How could she have denied offering me the chance to write a story for her magazine?

Had she made the denial, Terri wondered, in order to protect her, remembering her own advice not to 'tell', not to divulge anything to anyone about the storyline? But if she had, she surely wouldn't have added all that about those childhood fantasies of one day becoming a famous writer? And adding, making matters worse had Madge but known it, that she commissioned only professionals . . . and so on.

The worst part about it, Terri reflected sadly, was being unable to contact her, to tell her how, by that denial, she had totally wrecked her, Terri's, life.

Calling to the dog, she walked slowly back. Clive hailed her, walking across from the extension.

'Hi.' He smiled at her but received a blank look in answer. 'What's eating you?'

She had to put him off the scent and turned on a dazzling smile of her own, at which he rocked back on his heels. 'Wow. You could send a guy crazy with that smile of yours.'

He would never guess what it was costing her to keep it in place. 'Did you want something?' she asked.

'As a matter of fact, yes. Can I borrow the keys to Brendan's secret hideaway for half an hour? I know you've got a set because I saw you use them the other day. There's something I want to look up in one of his reference books. It'd save me the trip to the town library—that is, if they've got such an erudite work in stock.'

'Sorry, Clive. No keys.'

This time his smile was forced. 'I don't believe you. Stop playing, Terri. Give.' He had turned strangely serious. His hand slipped into her jacket pocket, but she shook free of it.

'They're not there, I tell you.'

'So where are they? Here?' This time he felt for her hips and slipped each hand into a trouser pocket. She slapped at his wrists but he did not withdraw them.

'Will you stop it?' she cried. 'They're not——'

Snippet, alerted by her raised voice, barked and snapped at Clive's heels.

'What are you after, Keston?' The words cut harshly across the noise. 'As if I didn't know. Is the lady proving difficult to persuade? Strange.' His look sliced into her. 'I have it from the lady's own lips that she wouldn't object to a trial run with another——'

'Stop it!' Terri shrieked, covering her ears and running, with Snippet at her heels, into the house and up to her room, where she barricaded the door.

I hate him, she thought, but her inner self told her, You love him more than you'll love any other man who might one day come into your life.

So where did that get her? she asked herself, staring down at the pile of hastily collected belongings strewn across the bed. There were so many books still on the bookshelves that she despaired of getting everything into the cases she had brought with her.

She realised with a jolt that, by leaving in this precipitate fashion, she was walking out on her real employer, without notice, without warning. But it had to be done. She'd have lost her job anyway, she reflected, as a result of last night's activities—she could not really apply the title 'lovemaking' to what had taken place between her and Brendan Stewart.

There was a distant ring of the telephone and Harvey's voice called urgently to her.

My sister? Terri wondered, running down to the hall, her heart lifting in anticipation, only to fall when Harvey told her, handing over the phone, 'Annie Macfarlane. She sounds as clear as if she were in this country.'

Which was precisely where the speaker was, Terri discovered, listening with growing dismay.

'Christiana needs to be in bed,' Annie was saying. 'She's got this chest infection and she's coughing badly. You're to drop everything, she says, and look after her. No nurse, only you. You're to tell her grandson that he must release you from the work he has given you——'

'That's easily done,' Terri informed her. Little did Mrs Stewart know just how easily, Terri reflected. 'I'm so sorry to hear that Mrs Stewart is ill. I'll come straight away and collect her——'

'No need, dear,' said Annie. 'We're hiring a taxi to bring us from the airport. It's a long way, but we should arrive by lunchtime.'

There was no alternative, Terri decided, but to seek out her employer's grandson and tell him the news. She found him seated at his desk in his office in the extension.

He looked up coolly, waiting for her to speak.

'Don't worry,' burst from her, 'I haven't come to plead for my job back.' An eyebrow flicked up, but otherwise he did not stir. 'I wouldn't have it if you offered it to me.'

Oh, God, she thought, this wasn't what she had come to tell him.

'I'm sorry.' She swallowed the lump that had irritatingly formed in her throat. 'It's about your grandmother. She's not well. They're back in this country. Annie Macfarlane telephoned just now.'

The blankness of his expression was wiped out by the news. He threw down his pencil. 'What's wrong with my grandmother?'

Terri explained. 'They're arriving around midday. She says she wants to go straight to bed.'

He pushed back the chair and rose. 'I'll hire a nurse.' He reached for the phone.

'No.' Terri's hand shot out to stop him, but she couldn't prevent her hand from touching his. Their eyes met, clashed, fought, then hers closed, hiding her despair. He did not toss her hand aside, just waited for her to remove it.

'Why not?' came sharply from him.

'Your grandmother specifically said no nurse. She wants me to look after her.'

He paused, dropped the phone, then lifted a shoulder, his face quite blank again. 'So be it.'

'Which means,' she felt impelled to add, 'that I won't be able to leave now. I'm sorry. I'll keep out of your way.' At the door, her lips broke free of her own restraint again. 'But I promise not to *snoop* and *spy* and ferret out secret documents.'

He was seated, tapping the pencil on the desk.

'And if you want to know what Clive Keston was really after, it wasn't what you assumed it was.' She paused.

'Well?' She really had his interest now.

'He wanted to borrow the keys he was convinced I still had to your cottage. He wanted to use one of your special reference books, he said.'

Brendan's eyes narrowed. 'Did he, now?'

She was about to go, when he said, 'Terri.' She could no more resist his command to stay than Snippet could resist a bone. 'Thank you for that piece of information. You don't know how important it is.'

'Does—does that make me a counter-spy?' she asked with a hint of irony. 'Or even a d-double agent?'

She allowed her eyes to meet his, but tore them away and withdrew from the room before that lump in her throat produced the tears which, ever since their terrible parting at the cottage, had threatened to appear every minute of every hour.

'Come over here, young woman.'

Christiana lay on pillows piled high, pale and heavy-eyed, but a little less tired than when she had arrived home two days before.

Terri turned from stacking the tray after her patient's meagre breakfast and obeyed her request. The gaze that inspected her was just a little too penetrating for her peace of mind.

'Tired,' said her employer, taking her hand, 'that is to be expected. I've asked a lot of you since my return. But dispirited, not to say a little depressed?' She shook her head. 'That does not go with your personality.' A puzzled frown was followed by an angry stare. 'You've changed. There's a look about you that was not there before.' She dropped Terri's hand. 'Send for my grandson at once.'

With fingers that trembled, Terri called Brendan's extension. On receiving a curt response, she said, 'I'm sorry to disturb you but your grandmother would like you to visit her.'

'At once,' came a chesty bark from behind her.

'I heard,' said Brendan on a note of weariness. A few minutes later, he came, his empty eyes resting momentarily on Terri. 'Yes, Grandmother?'

'You know why I've sent for you?' No doubting the patient's anger now. 'This girl.' Brendan's brows rose, but he did not look at the girl in question. 'And you. And don't look at me like that, Brendan. I'm too old to be fooled.' She rested on the pillows and closed her eyes. 'God knows, Terri, I should carry out my threat and dismiss you. I warned you. And as for you, Brendan, my instinct is to——'

'Cut me out of your will, Grandmother?' The tone was so weary, his grandmother opened her eyes. 'Or even——' his eyes skimmed Terri's face '—make me marry the girl?' He turned to Terri. 'Would you have me if I asked you?'

'If this is a proposal, no *thank* you. These days, as if you didn't know, sharing a—a bed with someone doesn't necessarily call for an offer of marriage.'

Christiana stirred agitatedly. 'I am *furious* with you, both of you. So go, *go*. But needless to say,' she added as they stood together at the door, 'I shall not carry out my threat, Terri. I need your help too much. However, it will take me a long, long time to forgive you. And you, Brendan.' She turned her cheek against the pillow.

Outside, Brendan detained Terri as she made for the stairs. 'Are you ill?'

'No, just tired. But thanks for your concern.' It hit her then. 'If you're worried about whether I'm——'

'I took precautions. I told you. But if——'

A series of angry barks broke out, accompanied by unmuffled curses. Terri dived for the kitchen, racing through it and rushing through the entrance to the extension.

Outside Brendan's office, Snippet had Clive by the trouser leg, eyes wide with snarling fury, a series of growls emanating from his throat.

'Let go, will you?' Clive was shouting. 'You miserable little——'

'Snippet,' Brendan barked back to the dog, 'leave. Leave, I say.'

The dog reluctantly released his victim who, pale with fright, was rubbing his ankle. 'The little——'

'Are you hurt?' Terri, concerned for Snippet's sake, as well as Clive's, crouched down to inspect Clive's ankle, pushing up the trouser leg while Brendan looked on. 'Thank heaven, no blood.' She glanced up at Clive's face. 'Are you OK?'

'Yeah, OK, no thanks to that little b——'

'Caught in the act, Keston?' Brendan asked with irony. 'Intending to search my room in my absence?'

Clive's face turning scarlet was sufficient answer.

'I'll have to co-opt the hound on to the team,' Brendan went on, heavily sarcastic. 'Employ him as a guard dog.' He picked up Snippet and stroked him. 'Thanks a lot, pal.'

He put him down and Terri bent to run her hand over the dog's coat, hiding her own face, which had turned red at the thoughts that had chased through her mind— of Brendan's hand on her own body that wonderful night, of his lips on her skin, roaming, audacious, exciting . . .

Brendan opened his office door. 'And look who you'd have found if you'd succeeded in trespassing.'

'Hi.' Drusilla, an unlighted cigarette to her mouth, was seated at Brendan's desk in Brendan's swivel chair. 'Just waiting, darling, for your return.' She replaced the cigarette in its packet and rose with studied grace, noting Clive's appearance. 'You look slightly, shall I say, distraught, Clive. Were you looking for me?'

Clive's smile became a grin. 'How did you guess? And, needless to say, I guessed right where I'd find you. After all, you and the boss——' he extended crossed fingers, his smile widening '—are like this, yes?'

Drusilla insinuated herself round the desk and linked her arm with Brendan's, smiling up into his face. 'But yes,' she breathed. 'Yes, darling?'

Brendan's answer was to smile, as he did so releasing himself from his colleague's hold. Terri could hardly bear to see their obvious familiarity with each other.

Clive moved to Terri's side. 'And thanks, honey, for being so concerned about my leg.' His arm went around her waist. 'We make a good pair, too, don't we?'

Because her heart was slowly disintegrating under the impact of the unmistakable togetherness of the man she loved and the woman who clearly meant a great deal to him, Terri allowed Clive's arm to stay around her.

She glanced at him. 'Snippet's teeth are sharp,' she commented with a falsely concerned frown. 'I thought he might have managed to puncture your skin.'

'Hey,' he remarked softly as he smiled at her, 'I think I've got myself a caring lady friend.'

The telephone cut into the brittle silence. Drusilla's hand went lazily out to answer. 'Miss Butler? Why, yes, Mrs Stewart, she's here.' She covered the mouthpiece. 'Your employer wants you.' Her sharp tones turned to honey again. 'She's on her way, Mrs Stewart. How remiss of her to leave you alone for so long, and you in poor health, too.'

To Terri's angry ears, smarting at Drusilla's attempt to remind her of her status, the receiver at the other end crashed down before Drusilla could replace hers. One up to Mrs Stewart, she thought, hurrying to do her employer's bidding.

'See you at the party,' Clive called. 'We'll make music together, huh?'

At which Snippet, racing in Terri's footsteps, paused and, to her amusement, snarled over his shoulder right on cue.

Clive's idea of 'making music', Terri discovered, was to dance as close as she allowed for part of the time, then to swing her madly back and forward to the sounds of the assorted instruments which, with their players' enthusiastic co-operation, supplied the Scottish dance tunes.

Breathless as she was, her eyes bright with the exhilaration of the movement and the rhythm, Clive took these as signs that she was enamoured of him to the exclusion of every other man in the room.

Now and then her glance strayed to Brendan, but the sight of him moving in such close proximity to Drusilla hurt her so much, she did her best to discipline her gaze and force it to remain on her partner.

Pleading tiredness, Terri found a seat and tapped her feet to the music, keeping her eyes riveted on the brightly dressed musicians. When people parted, apparently making way for a man who seemed, to her surprise and agitation, to be making a beeline for her, Terri Butler, she made to rise and melt into the crowd herself.

He was there, standing in front of her, before she could rise from her chair. His kilt was of Stewart tartan—*dress* tartan, Mrs Stewart had at some time explained—his whole attire adding to his stature and authority.

He towered above her, his hand extended. Its message was clear—Refuse me if you dare. She contemplated it, looked up at him, saw the resolution in his face and the hard lines of his jaw. There was nothing in the world that she wanted more than to be in his arms and she found herself obeying that hand's command and placing herself in front of him.

'If you'd said no,' his lips left their message on her tingling ear, 'you'd have got what you deserved.'

Her shivering form felt the impact of his words, her imagination leaping at the thought of what he might have demanded of her, and of what she would have given to him had he chosen to keep his promise.

Her eyes closed as his body moved against her, the music having turned romantic and persuasive. A warning from deep inside told her, Resist this man. He takes and never gives.

'You look tired,' he commented, holding her away.

'I'm so sorry,' she retorted, 'that my looks don't meet with your approval, but we can't all be beautiful and cool and wear slinky outfits like your lady friend.'

'Who said I don't approve of your looks?'

'You just said. You said I look tired which, translated, means dull and uninspiring and most definitely a turn-off.'

'Yeah?' His eyes dipped to the cleft revealed by her low-cut white blouse. His hand slid to clamp around her hips, which tensed beneath her tight-fitting white skirt. 'A turn-off, you think?'

'Yes, I think. A woman to take away with you, Barry said, and another woman to come back to. Well, count me out, Brendan Stewart. After all, I'm not on the level, am I? I tell untruths about myself, I mislead deliberately so that——'

Her words were cut off by his punishing kiss. 'Shut up.' His message, stroking her lips, made her limbs begin to melt, her heart to pound.

She forced her eyes to stray, hoping to cool the heat that was beginning to sweep unchecked through her being. There was Clive, dancing boisterously again, this time with Drusilla.

'Fantasising that Keston's your dancing partner?' Brendan clipped, his finger flicking her cheek.

The action stung, which was, she knew, what he had intended. She pulled away, staring up at him. 'Just as you're no doubt fantasising that Drusilla is in your arms instead of me, Terri Butler, deceiver, spy and counter-spy.'

'Brendan, my pet...' Drusilla was alongside them, and she slid from Clive's hold, pushing between Terri and the man she really wanted.

Clive held out his arms, but Terri spun round and made for the kitchen.

'Harvey,' she said, her voice thick with threatening tears, 'I know that officially I'm a guest tonight, but—well, is there anything useful I could be doing?'

'Nae, lass. Go and enjoy yourself.'

She smiled and, when his back was turned, she slipped through the door and out of the extension, making for the house. The kitchen, as she had expected, was empty except for the dog, who nosed around her feet, tail wagging, then returned sleepily to his basket.

Mrs Stewart had also settled for the night, having first imperiously told her secretary to attend the party, even though she now had no working connection with the research team.

Making some tea, Terri sat drinking it in the rocking-chair, trying to forget the picture of Brendan dancing with Drusilla. Rinsing her cup, she returned to the chair and from nowhere came tears—of hopelessness, of love unreturned and likely to remain so; of her inability, through loyalty to and compassion for her employer, to remove herself physically and finally from the presence of the man who was the cause of her unhappiness.

Snippet leapt on to her lap as if sensing her distress and once again his coat grew damp from the droplets that descended on to him. He did not seem to mind, and curled up, sleeping again.

The door behind her opened. Assuming it was Harvey returning, she didn't turn.

'Why,' asked Brendan, closing the door, 'the mad dash from the revelry? Or did you make a date with Keston to meet him here, then take him up to your room unobserved?'

Her head jerked round. If he'd been nearer, she knew she would have hit out at him. 'Maybe *you* have arranged a tryst with your lady friend, and you're annoyed that I've spoiled your night of love?'

'Terri...' His voice held a soft rebuke, but his words stung. 'If I had, I wouldn't have brought her over here. I also have a room in the extension.'

She knew what he was implying. 'You——' she wished her lips wouldn't tremble so '—you know it all, don't you, all the answers, all the moves? Which goes with your lifestyle, doesn't it? Any available woman will do to appease your *manly* appetite.'

He did not answer, just moved round to look down at her. 'Even in this half-light——' she had turned on only one of the kitchen lights '—I can see that you look tired. OK, so I said it earlier—not, please note, to demean your looks as you thought, but as a statement of fact. You're working too hard looking after my grandmother.' He had, she noticed, not without a twinge of regret, changed out of his kilt.

'It's my job.'

'Not, however, to get tired to the point of collapse. I intend, with or without permission from the patient, to hire a nurse.'

Terri sat forward, the chair going with her, spilling Snippet on to the floor. 'But——'

Brendan's raised hand stopped her protest. 'A nurse to come morning and evening. Hi, hound.' He stooped to stroke the dog, then lifted his hand to the light. 'Damp. Why?' It took him about two seconds to work it out and he rubbed his hand on his hip, placing it and his other hand on the wooden arms of the chair. It threw her forward. 'So you've been crying. You really would have preferred Keston to me?'

It was her turn to stay silent. If she'd spoken, she would not have been able to guard her tongue and by now he would know how she preferred this man to any man on earth and always would.

'Sorry about spoiling your assignation, but——' he grasped her wrists and swung her up, taking the chair himself and pulling her on to his lap '—I'm the guy who's turned up in his place. The last I saw of him he was in Drusilla's fair embrace on the dance-floor.'

Her body curled to fit in with his shape, her head finding itself a heavenly resting place on his shoulder. His arms went round her and he rocked them both, his breath stirring strands of her hair, his hands shifting to cup her breasts.

Oh, how I love you . . . The words almost escaped her control. She could not prevent her body from arousing itself from its torpor, her pulses from leaping, the ache

low down in her stomach from crying out its message
to him—Take me, take me!

The rocking motion, the way her body was cupped by
his, created once again a sensation of tranquillity. In spite
of everything, she slept.

Wakening in the darkness, she found she was in her
own bed, her outerwear having been removed and the
covers drawn over her. She felt her face grow warm as
she realised just who had half undressed her.

Her outstretched hand told her that she was alone.
How could she have been otherwise? He had a bedroom
over there to which he could at any time invite Drusilla
and, on leaving her, Terri, here, had no doubt done so.

It was three days later that Terri saw Brendan again.
They met outside her employer's bedroom after Terri
had seen the lady doctor to her car.

Brendan wore a collared, short-sleeved woven black
shirt and well-fitting trousers to match. Through the unbuttoned neck a tiny area of hair showed and Terri had
to take a tight grip on her emotions as she recalled how,
when they had made love, she had rubbed her cheek
against that dark mat on his chest.

'Thank you,' she found herself saying, 'for lightening
my workload.'

Unsmiling, he nodded.

'The nurse, she's great. So efficient.'

He nodded again.

'And—and thank you for—for putting me to bed the
other night. And for—um—not taking advantage of
my——' she cleared her throat '—fatigue to—well...'

He inclined his head.

'This,' he said with a hint of mischief, 'is a very interesting, wide-ranging discussion we're having.'

Their eyes met, held, then laughter bubbled from her
throat, at which point he joined in.

'You two.' The voice from the bedroom was stronger now. 'What's going on between you?'

Terri preceded Brendan into the room. 'We were talking, Mrs Stewart, that's all.'

'Discussing my good points, Grandmother—how helpful and philanthropic I am. Not to mention,' he added with a mocking glance at Terri, 'how restrained and in control of my natural instincts I am.'

Christiana sighed, lying back on her pillows. 'In my state of health, Brendan, I can't even begin to understand the underlying meanings and innuendoes of your generation.'

A stride took him to her bedside, his hand covering hers where it lay on the bedcovers. 'Are you still not feeling well?' Would he ever, Terri wondered, show such devotion to any other woman?

'I've made great strides. Soon I'll be well enough to be up and about again. And,' she said with a loving smile, 'to put you, young man, well and truly in your place.'

The distant ring of the telephone had him listening. When Harvey summoned him, calling up the stairs, he went fast, sketching a salute to his grandmother and throwing an ironic smile in Terri's direction.

He erupted into the room again as Terri was about to leave her employer to take a brief rest.

Without explanation, he addressed Terri. 'I want a meeting arranged at once. The whole team is to assemble in the usual place in——' he consulted his watch '—half an hour.'

Christiana stared at her grandson as if she were seeing him for the first time.

'I don't work for you any more,' Terri reminded him, nonplussed. 'The lady who took my place——'

'You were never replaced. Drusilla took on the secretarial work.' He turned away, then turned back. 'Will you do as I ask?' he said, coldly now. 'And I want you at the meeting, too.'

'But——'

'Please excuse me, Grandmother.' Then he was gone.

'My dear child,' Christiana said, aghast, 'why do you let him talk to you like that? You let me believe he has made love to you——'

'He has, Mrs Stewart,' Terri whispered.

'He's held you in his arms, kissed you, not to mention——' She checked herself. 'Yet he addresses you as if you were the dust beneath his feet?'

'He doesn't trust me, Mrs Stewart.'

'Doesn't *trust* you? I state categorically that you are the most trustworthy young woman I have ever come across. And I propose to tell him so.'

Shaking her head, Terri told her, 'It wouldn't make any difference. It's connected with the project the team is working on.'

'What can *you* know about that? Your career, your references make no mention of scientific research.'

Terri explained about her academic grades in relevant subjects. 'Some of what they're saying I understand, but not that much.' She had to end the discussion. 'Mrs Stewart——' she smoothed the bedclothes '—please have your rest. It's of no consequence how Brendan t-talks to me.'

She cursed her faltering words.

'You love him, Terri?'

'I——' She had to clear her throat. 'Much good does it do me,' she answered with a gallant attempt at a smile.

The round, only faintly wrinkled face had lost some colour. 'I did warn you, my dear. But,' she sighed, 'who can prevent a foolish heart from transferring itself into another's keeping?'

In her office, Terri picked up the internal phone and contacted the members of the team, each of whom showed surprise, and, like her, puzzlement.

Fifteen minutes later Brendan walked into the meeting-room and took his place at the table beside Terri, clearly the only thing on his mind being the reason for the un-expected summons to the meeting.

'About an hour ago,' he announced, 'I received a phone call from a contact in London.' He looked at his colleagues one by one, disconcertingly including Terri in his penetrating scrutiny. 'The trials of our drug—someone taking part is registering an adverse effect.'

CHAPTER TWELVE

DISBELIEVING groans were followed by a series of 'oh, no's and 'oh, hell's.

Brendan proceeded to go into technical details, some of which Terri was able to understand. She also grasped how serious the matter was if the one negative result was reproduced in others.

Clive and Drusilla exchanged rueful glances.

'Back to the drawing-board,' sighed Barry Henderson.

'Not that far back, surely?' exclaimed George Smythe.

'Probably just a matter of holding our horses, yes, boss?' queried Bill Parton. 'Await events? Fingers firmly crossed?'

Brendan nodded. 'Now do you see the sense behind my reluctance to publish too soon?' His question was mainly directed at Clive, with whom and on which subject, Terri recollected, he had crossed swords not so long ago.

Clive made a face and lifted his shoulders.

'So the celebratory party was somewhat premature,' Drusilla remarked, carefully using an eraser on her notebook and brushing it clean.

'Our rivals, it appears, are still behind us,' Brendan told her, 'but catching up fairly fast, or so I'm told.'

'Our spies have been busy, then?' Clive commented.

Terri's heart jolted uncomfortably at the word and she became conscious of Brendan's eyes upon her.

I didn't do it, she wanted to shout, whatever it is I'm supposed to have done. I'm innocent of any charge that you might bring against me. But the words stayed locked in her mind.

'You could say that,' Brendan answered with a touch of irony.

She looked down to discover that her hand had picked up her pencil and was in the process of writing the message which a few minutes earlier her brain had not allowed her to speak.

A hand reached out and the notebook was pulled from her grasp. Eyes scanned the message, then the notebook was passed back. Anxiously she studied Brendan's features. Those eyes were cynical, the mouth just a little twisted.

Well, her hand had done its best to exonerate her, but she could have told it it was wasting its time.

The meeting broke up and Terri escaped back to the house. In her office, she sat at her desk, reading again the message she had written in her notebook. No matter how much she protested her innocence, Brendan wouldn't believe her. If only she could talk to her sister, ask her why she'd let her down so badly when Brendan had attempted to verify her claim about writing a story.

She could try reaching her, couldn't she, through the magazine? Maybe they had a number by now through which Madge could be contacted?

'They're home,' Madge's deputy told her.

Terri's heart soared. 'Home? Then can I speak to her?'

'Sorry,' was the answer.

'*Please*. After all, I am her sister.'

'Terri, is it a matter of life and death?'

Almost, she thought, but she had to be honest. 'Not exactly.'

'Sorry, Terri. Madge has given strict instructions not to be disturbed until further notice. It seems that she and Leslie have gone into a kind of hiding. They're not only jet-lagged, but exhausted, too. Sorry,' she repeated. 'Try again in a few days.'

A call to Madge and Leslie's home produced only the irritatingly bright voice of the answering machine. In her own room, she opened a drawer and pulled out the pages on which she had scribbled the outline of her story.

It seemed OK, she told herself with just a little satisfaction. Most of all, it needed finishing, so why not now? Sighing, she pushed it away.

Not only had her enthusiasm gone, her heart wasn't in it any longer. It couldn't be, could it, she asked herself despairingly, since she'd placed it, so stupidly, and so totally, into Brendan Stewart's fickle keeping?

Each day Terri's hand stretched out to pick up the phone, only to draw back. Once, she actually rang Madge's office, only to receive the same off-putting reply. And that darned machine at their home, she thought, if it answers me once more, I'll tell it exactly what I think of it.

Christiana, being back to her normal health, dined every evening with her secretary. Sometimes, Brendan joined them. It was after one such occasion that he pushed back his chair and looked at Terri.

'I'm going for a walk and I want you to come with me.'

Christiana glanced from one to the other, eyes expectant and, Terri noticed, hopeful.

'Oh, but——'

'You are coming with me.' Each word was stated clearly, the authoritative tone clouding the hope in his grandmother's face.

'Get your coat, dear,' Christiana said, glancing out and plainly trying to make the best of the situation. 'It's a lovely evening, but a bit windy. You and Brendan— you'll enjoy the walk.'

Later, Terri had to agree. She was enjoying the walk, with Snippet racing and sniffing and hiding and reappearing. The breeze was bracing, the sun slow to set, the hills around them growing darker and grander as the minutes passed.

'I've spoken to your brother-in-law.'

She stared at him. 'My *brother-in-law*?'

'That's what I said.'

The Atlantic Ocean frothed against the rocky shoreline, the cottages across the bay picked up the sunset's glow.

'So?' Her heart's pace had nothing to do with the gradient which their feet were negotiating. 'Did he confirm what I told you?' No answer. 'About my writing a story, being on the level?'

'I didn't even ask. He did the talking.'

Terri's heartbeats slowed. 'But why? I mean, how? I've never mentioned you to him.'

'I told you, while I was in London, I contacted his magazine, having failed to make contact with your sister. At that time, the subject you've just referred to *was* on my mind.'

'And now it isn't?'

He didn't even bother to answer. 'He rang me here, this evening. I'd left my number.'

'But why didn't he ask to speak to me? I've been trying for days to contact them——'

'He told me,' Brendan went on as if she had not spoken, 'that he had received some information through a scientific-based news agency he had never heard of. A piece for publication, he said, about a certain drug——'

'Oh, no! Yours?' she asked, aghast. 'About the project you're all working on? But you've ruled against publication yet. I've heard you say it over and over again.'

'Nevertheless——' his hard profile was etched against the pearl-blue sky '—someone has taken it upon themselves to jump the gun and release a report in advance of the completion of the trials. And I want to know who.'

His jaw was set, his eyes narrowed as they scanned the wild landscape.

'It wasn't me,' she declared, her voice high. 'Please believe me.'

There was a long pause as they kept on walking. Then Brendan said, 'Leslie gave me the two names that were attached to the report. Two men—Drew James and Kes Clivton. I told him I'd never heard of them.'

'Employees of your rivals?' Terri offered.

'Hardly. Whoever they are,' he said through his teeth, 'I'll get them and I'll——' He clamped his mouth over the words he had plainly censored for her benefit.

'I thanked Leslie for warning me, asked him to suppress the report until further notice from me. He agreed. Not only was it not official, I told him, it was premature, in view of the doubt that's been hanging over the trials.'

His hand brushed against hers, taking hold of it, and Terri felt blinded by sunbeams, as if the sun were rising instead of sinking. All of her body came alarmingly alive and she wanted to turn to him and shout her love for him so loudly that her declaration echoed back from the mountains all around.

When he turned her and held her shoulders, looking deep into her eyes, she had no resistance left with which to fight his arms as they took her into them; nor even the slightest desire to evade his lips as they lowered to claim hers as their own.

'Give.' The word came from deep in his throat. 'You know what I want.'

'Brendan, no,' she answered hoarsely.

'Brendan, yes,' he countered, forcing her backwards so that her knees buckled and she dropped to the ground. He came down to her, one hand at her throat, forcing up her head, the other behind it so that her mouth had to take all he was giving it... and taking from it.

'Not here,' she whispered. 'It's too public.'

He lifted his head and shouted a laugh, looking round. 'All these people around us, they're crowding us, cramping our style! Come on, baby.' His mouth was on

hers again, invading, compelling. 'There's not a human
being in sight.'

'Snippet,' she managed.

Another laugh, then his hand, which had been busy
unzipping her jacket, slid beneath her sweater, slipping
off the shoulder-straps of her bra and taking over her
breasts, one by one, moulding and caressing and roughly
grasping each in turn.

Her gasp he took into his own system, drawing her
breath into his lungs. Her arms twisted round his neck,
pulling instead of doing their duty and pushing. Instead
of stiffening, her body arched, invited . . .

It was Snippet's frantic barking that brought them
back to earth. With a curse that he did not bother to
smother, Brendan lay momentarily against her, then got
to his feet.

'What now, hound? For Pete's sake, don't you have
any diplomacy, any consideration for——?' The dog,
Terri saw, rousing herself and putting her clothes to
rights, was facing across the inlet, his small figure rigid
with canine annoyance.

From his pocket, Brendan produced his binoculars,
raising them to his eyes. 'There's a light in my cottage.
Do *you* know anything about this?'

'Me? Why should I?' Where had the lover gone?
Disappeared, not even lurking behind the angry eyes,
the set mouth. Vanished, with the sun. And the coolness
it had left behind chilled her to the core. 'Oh, God,
Brendan, do you really think that badly of me?'

He looked her over, eyes hooded. 'OK. Come with
me.'

He began to run, back where they had come from,
down the hill, half balancing on pieces of rock. Snippet
preceded him, while Terri followed them both.

By the side of the inlet, Brendan untied his boat.
'Come,' he said again, his hand steadying Terri as she

stepped in, while Snippet made himself comfortable at
her feet.

'Damn the outboard motor for not working,' he
muttered.

'The light's moving,' she told him as, with his back
to the cottage, he rowed them across. 'Brendan...' she
was frightened now '...who could it be?'

'Some thieving, nosy swine,' he snapped, his concentration deep as he forced his arms to work even faster.

Across the inlet he leapt on to the shore, pausing
briefly to help Terri to disembark, then hauling the boat
clear of the water. He walked swiftly and soundlessly
towards the cottage entrance. Following him, Terri
scooped up Snippet, hiding his nose under her arm to
prevent him from barking. As they approached, Terri
picked up the sound of the generator.

Brendan burst in, looking right and left. Switching on
the lights as he went, he strode across to his private office,
flinging open the door. Two people crouched there,
dazzled by the sudden illumination, while two hand-
lanterns sat side by side on the desk. These, Terri deduced, had clearly been the source of the moving lights
which she and Brendan had seen as they had climbed.

'You thieving bastard,' rasped Brendan, 'get out of
here.'

Clive, face draining of colour, dropped the files he
was holding.

'As for you——' he turned to Clive's accomplice,
whose arms were deep inside the cabinet itself '——I'd like
to wring your swan-like neck.'

Drusilla, more discomposed than Terri had ever seen
her, rose shakily from her knees. Her hand lifted to rest
on Brendan's shoulder.

'Darling, I—I was trying to protect your papers from
this—this——' Unable to find a suitably derogatory
word, she gestured towards the other man.

Brendan seized her hand and threw it from him.

'Liar, Dru,' Clive hit out. 'You're in this as deep as I am.'

Which explained, Terri reflected, the way she had seen them reading each other's notes, the odd arm-length familiarity which seemed to exist between them.

'And you, Terri——' the smile Clive switched on was intended to dazzle '—I can't thank you enough for telling me where I could find the stuff I wanted. All along you've co-operated——'

'Now who's lying?' Terri cried. 'When you tried to get the keys to this place from me, I wouldn't let you have them. Do you call *that* co-operating? Brendan, you just have to believe . . .'

'Kes Clivton.' Brendan rolled the name around his tongue and commented reflectively, 'A kind of anagram? The answer being *Clive Keston*. Do you deny that, Keston?'

Clive's face paled further still. 'Who the hell gave that away? No, don't tell me, it was *her* brother-in-law, the rat.' He stabbed the air in Terri's direction. 'He always was teacher's pet; I remember from our schooldays. I should have known he'd pass it back to source.'

'All Leslie Cowley told me,' Brendan took him up, 'was that something that sounded like a spoof agency had *released* the information. An exclusive to his magazine only, or so that non-existent scientific agency alleged.'

'Brendan.' Terri's eyes widened as an idea came to her. 'Did you say the other person's name was—Drew James?'

He frowned. 'I did.' He picked up Terri's train of thought and his head swung to the right. 'Drusilla Jameson . . . Drew James, right?'

'Oh, darling——' her hands closed around his arm '—I didn't mean any harm, honest. I agreed with Clive. I just thought it was time we published.'

Brendan's lips almost disappeared. 'Without the knowledge or consent of the project leader—myself? Not to mention the other members of the team, who had every right to be consulted on the subject?'

Drusilla's head dropped into her hands. 'Forgive me, Brendan, darling. We've meant so much to each other...'

'Get out, you and your miserable partner in crime.'

Snippet wriggled so much that Terri let him down, at which he proceeded to break into a series of deafening barks, accompanied by a furious snapping of teeth in the vicinity of Clive's ankles.

Clive's exit was satisfyingly rapid. The dog then turned his attention to Drusilla, sitting on his haunches and alternately barking and growling until she snatched up her bag, lantern and jacket and fled from the room.

The silence that followed was almost as deafening as the noise that had preceded it. Snippet returned, tail wagging as if he recognised how completely he had vanquished the foe. He disappeared into the living-room and began to reacquaint himself with its contents.

Terri crouched to gather the files and papers, partly through training and partly to avoid Brendan's eyes. But he disconcerted her by joining in, his face only a hand's stretch from hers.

'How did they get in?' she asked to break the silence. 'And what did they think they'd find here?'

'They forced a window. I noticed as I came in. As for what they were looking for, I imagine it was a desperate search for an update on the results of the trials. Maybe they had a twinge of conscience and thought, a bit late in the day, that they'd better do a bit of checking up on the subject and if necessary ask your brother-in-law to put the "report" they'd sent him on hold. Which, of course, as I told you, I did when I spoke to him.'

'You mean they thought they might find the information here, so as to avoid having to identify themselves when asking at source what was happening?'

He nodded. 'That "source" wouldn't have told them, anyway, not even if they'd used their real names instead of their assumed names. The information was available only to me as project leader.'

'At that meeting you asked me to attend, you told them, didn't you, that there was a question mark over the trials?'

'Right. I heard this evening, again in strictest confidence, that it was a false alarm.'

Terri looked up eagerly. 'So everything's going OK?'

'Very OK.'

'Do you,' she said, her voice thick with emotion, 'believe what Clive said about my co-operating with him? Because he was lying, Brendan, he was lying.'

'OK, so he was lying,' he agreed without expression. 'That doesn't mean he meant nothing to you.'

'All right,' she felt compelled to hit back, 'so you can't believe your precious Drusilla was two-timing not only you but all your colleagues. You're so infatuated with her good looks——'

'What good looks?'

Slowly, Terri straightened, finding herself staring into Brendan's narrowed eyes.

'Don't be silly, she's beautiful, she's brainy, she's got it all——'

The telephone rang, almost jumping off the desk. Thank heaven for that, Terri found herself thinking; I was almost sending him flying after her to get her back again.

'Terri Butler?' Brendan listened. 'Yes, she's here.' He handed the receiver over.

'Yes? Madge? Oh, *Madge*. Am I glad to hear from you!'

'I'm told you've been chasing me all over the world.'

'Oh, why, Madge, *why* did you deny knowing anything when Brendan asked you if it was true that you'd given me a commission to write a story for your magazine? You know as well as I do——'

'Why? Because Clive——'

'Clive Keston?' She looked up to find Brendan's hooded gaze on her and could not hide her dismay.

'The same. He rang a while ago to tell us about the coincidence of meeting you in Scotland and described how furious you were when you realised that we had told him about your writing that story. So we, Leslie and I, decided that in future we'd deny everything where that was concerned. OK?'

'No, not OK. It was *Brendan* who wanted to know, that's why. He's suspected me all this time of being— well, a kind of industrial spy. He thought I'd come here to steal all his secrets, or rather the team's secrets——'

'You're not making sense, little sister. What team? Football team?'

Terri couldn't help laughing. '*Research* team, idiot. Brendan's right here. Will you *please* now tell him the truth?'

'It's that important? Hey, Terri, I haven't been messing up your love life, have I?'

Brendan had clearly heard Madge's part of the conversation and took the phone from Terri's moist hand.

'You darned nearly have, Mrs Cowley. OK—Madge. So tell me about that story—it's true? Not,' he said with his eyes on Terri, 'that it matters any more. True or not, it won't change my opinion of your little sister.' He listened. 'So it's true, which means I've got a budding author on my hands.

'Yes,' he agreed with another thousand-volt flash in Terri's direction, 'we'll keep you informed. Terri says goodbye. And thanks.'

Step over step took him towards her. She started to back away, only to realise that once again her legs were out of phase with her thought processes. So she stood her ground.

Hands pushed into the waistband of his trousers, he raked her with his gaze.

'What was all that,' he asked, 'about Drusilla's good looks?'

'I've—I'm——' She took a deep breath. 'I'm afraid I've forgotten.'

He laughed, still keeping his distance.

'What did you mean by saying,' she asked, 'that, no matter what Madge told you about whether or not I was writing a story, it wouldn't change your opinion of me?' He merely smiled. 'Is it so bad you won't tell me?'

'For the second time—I just have to get this straight—Keston means nothing to you?'

'I told you, he means *nothing*. How could he when——?' Careful, she cautioned herself. You almost gave your feelings away. 'But you and Drusilla?'

'You want honesty? OK. Once, there was something between us, but she wanted more than I was prepared to give.'

'So it ended?' Why was her heart sinking so? Terri wondered. She knew the score. Hadn't he spelt it out when they had first met? Bliss without the wedded . . .

'It ended, although she kept hoping the affair would revive.'

'Didn't you ever suspect *her* motives as well as Clive's?'

'It wasn't long before I began to link them. I noticed their whispered comments, their nods and shakes of the head. So, yes, I did begin to suspect her, too.'

Terri nodded, secretly glad that their behaviour had attracted his attention just as it had attracted hers.

'Now . . .' he considered her ' . . . that other question: my opinion of you.'

He still made no move and Terri bent down to continue tidying up.

'Don't you want to know what it is?' he asked.

'It—it might be useful when—when I'm applying for another job. Which means——' she pretended to concentrate on the scattered papers '—I'd want it in writing. Anyway...' she looked over the length of him as he towered over her, long legs a little apart, hands in pockets '...I know what you think of me. You believe that some unknown company with a research team of its own planted me here to steal your team's secrets and help the company claim the prize ahead of you. You think I'm a spy——'

He crouched to join her as she knelt. His finger tipped her chin. 'At first, maybe I did. I thought it was too much of a coincidence that a girl of your intelligence and educational background just happened to apply to work for my grandmother.'

'Coincidences do happen,' she argued. 'Look at how Clive turned up here, quite by chance finding that I was working here.'

'I thought at the time that that was part of the conspiracy.' He straightened. 'After all, I did see you peering through the windows of my cottage that first day we met.'

'Curiosity, pure and simple,' she told him.

'To me you looked as if you meant business. For a long time I couldn't work out whether you were male or female.' He smiled. 'After all, you were wearing my clothes.'

She smiled back. 'You win that one.'

'You do understand that I had to be on my guard? So much of the team's work depended on keeping our secrets well away from our rivals' grasping hands. And on not being published too soon in the science journals. Believe me, in the scientific world the gloves are off when it comes to a first in many fields of research.'

Terri nodded. 'You mean with taking out patents and things. I understand all that.'

'So you also understand why I've been so suspicious? I had no evidence that Keston was anything but on the level, but something told me not to trust him completely. Which was one of the reasons why I was so—shall we say?—concerned about whether you and he——'

'Were in collusion—partners in crime, because we both knew Leslie, who was—is—the editor of a science magazine? And who, as I told you once,' she conceded, 'asked to be kept informed of any new scientific developments, so that he could be the first to publish.' She shook her head. 'It's strange, but I never quite trusted Clive, either. When,' she ventured, 'did you begin to trust me?'

'I started to believe in your innocence when you told me about writing that story, but all that was held in abeyance when your sister denied all knowledge of it.'

'But now you've heard her explanation of that denial, you accept that I never intended to deceive you or anyone else?' Even if he did accept it, she warned her hopeful self, it didn't follow that his lovemaking meant any more to him than a means of satisfying his desire.

He lifted her to her feet and looked for a long time into her eyes. 'After a while—a surprisingly short while—the anger I felt that you might be an industrial spy was tempered by another, warmer feeling.'

Warmer? Yes, she could understand that. As a woman she might have attracted him, but that was all.

A yelp brought a curse to his lips.

'Snippet wants out,' Terri said.

Brendan's hands dropped away and he went through the living-room to open the outer door. Terri removed her jacket and went on tidying up. Brendan must have gone out, too, probably to secure the boat to its mooring.

They both returned and there was the sound of scurrying paws.

'Come down, hound,' Brendan shouted.

'I'll get him.' Terri dashed up the stairs and found that Snippet had leapt on to Brendan's bed. 'No dogs in bedrooms,' she scolded, throwing herself across the bed and grabbing hold of the wiry body, then depositing him on the floor. 'Don't you remember that rule?'

'So *you* remembered?' Brendan regarded her from the doorway.

'From last time?' Colour invaded her cheeks. 'Yes, I remembered.'

'Downstairs, dog,' Brendan ordered and Snippet reluctantly obeyed. Quietly the door was closed and Terri made to rise from the bed. 'Don't get up.'

Resting on her elbow, she looked up at him. 'Why not?'

'Provoking me, hmm? *I* am remembering something else.' He approached her, speaking softly. 'The way we shared this bed. The way I felt about that beautiful girl lying beside me. And yet—Grandmother's orders—I couldn't touch her. But tonight, lady, it's different.' He dropped down beside her. 'We're going to share it again. Also, there's a little unfinished business we're going to transact.'

'But——' It was only token resistance, and they both knew it.

'No buts. And this time I'll tolerate no interference from my much loved grandparent.' He drew her across and on to his lap and his arms closed round her, the pressure of his mouth against hers forcing her downwards until she lay on her back.

He rolled over and on to her, his mouth still on hers, possessive and forceful. Then he lifted himself away, gazing into her eyes. He stroked back her hair, trailing his fingers around her throat.

'Seven days, I said, didn't I, seemed like seven years? How do you think I've been feeling recently, with all my instincts and urges telling me to make love to you again, but with circumstances conniving to stop me from doing just that?'

Instincts, urges. That was all he was offering. But if this was to be an affair, short though it might be, because before long she'd have to leave and seek other work—how could she stay there, loving him so much?— then she would accept making love with him, without the loving—and the consequences—with arms outstretched.

He removed her layers of clothing one by one, kissing each bared part of her body as he uncovered it. Then he slowly divested himself of his own clothes, after which they lay together, flesh to flesh. She was able to utter not a single word of protest.

He caressed and stroked with hand and mouth and found places that made her body surrender itself entirely to the pleasure he was giving her. Throwing aside any inhibitions that might even then have been lingering, she finally abandoned all restraint and moved ecstatically to the rhythm he dictated, losing herself totally in the great eruption of joy that swept through her entire being and which bound them as though they were truly one.

When the telephone rang he groaned against her breast, then lifted himself from her to go to answer its summons. In spite of everything, he smiled as he talked.

'Yes, Grandmother, she's here with me. In bed, Grandmother; does that shock you? You're pleased? I'll tell her. She loves me?' He frowned. 'You're psychic, telepathic? She told *you*, before she's told *me*?'

His eyes slewed round to rest on Terri's recumbent, throbbing figure. 'I'll—no, Grandmother, I won't tell you what I'll do to her for that little omission. You can guess? Grandmother! Yes, of course we're going to be married.'

Terri sprang up, pulling the covers around her. 'Who said?'

'She doesn't want to marry me, Grandmother.'

Terri dashed across and wrested the phone from his grasp. 'Of course I do, Mrs Stewart. But he hasn't asked me. Bliss without the wedded, he once said. No commitment.'

'Not until I met the right woman,' he said in the background.

'If he asks me will I say yes?' Terri went on, success-fully evading Brendan's straying, possessive hand. 'Of course I will.' She laughed delightedly. 'This is the fun-niest proposal of marriage I've ever come across. A kind of three-way link-up.' She listened. 'Yes, of course I'll call you Grandmother. As of now? Yes,' she said softly. 'Grandmother. We can be married from your house? Oh, Mrs—Grandmother, that would be wonderful.'

She listened again and rang off. 'Your grandmother asked me to tell you not to worry about her. She'll be off again, she says, just as soon as she's fit. This time, she and Annie Macfarlane will make for the southern hemisphere, and nothing you might say to her, she said, will stop her.'

Brendan laughed resignedly, shaking his head. When his impatient arms came out, Terri went into them with eagerness and joy.

In the night, she stirred. Her story was beginning to write itself. Easing from the bed, she pulled on Brendan's robe and slipped downstairs. In the office she found a pencil and a large notepad.

Going into the living-room, she curled up on the sofa and Snippet's tail wagged twice in sleepy greeting. For a while she wrote fiercely, her hand scarcely able to keep up with her thoughts.

There was a shout from upstairs. 'Where's my woman? Terri, where the hell have you gone?' She stopped writing. The anguish mixed in with the anger told her all she wanted to know, would ever need to know, about his deep and fundamental need of her.

'Darling,' she called back, 'I'm down here.'

He appeared at the door, shirt hanging loose. She smiled at him radiantly. 'Your "woman" has finally turned into an author. Brendan,' she added delightedly, 'I've got a storyline at last!'

Head thrown back, he laughed. 'Took you long enough. What is it? Or is that breaking your strictest rule never to tell?'

She shook her head, her dishevelled hair swinging. 'You're an exception to my rule.'

'Thanks, my love, for the compliment.'

'Well, it's about us. About me meeting you. And——' should she tell him? '—falling in love with you.' He looked gratified. 'And about you meeting me——'

'Snap. And falling in love with you.'

'You did?' she asked wonderingly.

'At first sight. With the girl lying asleep on the shore, oblivious of the storm, her hair tangled, with a face I'd only ever seen in my dreams. And her body so vulnerable I wanted to gather it up and never let it go.'

Her eyes caught the light from his.

'And then,' she continued, 'we——' She stopped, frowning.

'Writer's block?'

She nodded.

'And then,' he took her up, 'my beautiful piece of driftwood from the ocean out there——' his arms scooped her up bodily '—come with me and I'll show you what happened next.'

And, carrying her up the stairs again, he proceeded to do so in the minutest, most ecstatic detail.

In the rising gale the ocean flung itself against the rocky shore, the windows rattled, the wind howled around the cottage, but they didn't hear a thing.

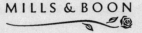

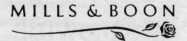

Cruel Legacy

One man's untimely death deprives a wife of her husband, robs a man of his job and offers someone else the chance of a lifetime...

Suicide — the only way out for Andrew Ryecart, facing crippling debt. An end to his troubles, but for those he leaves behind the problems are just beginning, as the repercussions of this most desperate of acts reach out and touch the lives of six different people — changing them forever.

Special large-format paperback edition

OCTOBER
£8.99

WORLDWIDE

Next Month's Romances

Each month you can choose from a wide variety of romance with Mills & Boon. Below are the new titles to look out for next month, why not ask either Mills & Boon Reader Service or your Newsagent to reserve you a copy of the titles you want to buy – just tick the titles you would like and either post to Reader Service or take it to any Newsagent and ask them to order your books.

Please save me the following titles:

	Please tick	✓
TRIAL BY MARRIAGE	*Lindsay Armstrong*	
ONE FATEFUL SUMMER	*Margaret Way*	
WAR OF LOVE	*Carole Mortimer*	
A SECRET INFATUATION	*Betty Neels*	
ANGELS DO HAVE WINGS	*Helen Brooks*	
MOONSHADOW MAN	*Jessica Hart*	
SWEET DESIRE	*Rosemary Badger*	
NO TIES	*Rosemary Gibson*	
A PHYSICAL AFFAIR	*Lynsey Stevens*	
TRIAL IN THE SUN	*Kay Thorpe*	
IT STARTED WITH A KISS	*Mary Lyons*	
A BURNING PASSION	*Cathy Williams*	
GAMES LOVERS PLAY	*Rosemary Carter*	
HOT NOVEMBER	*Ann Charlton*	
DANGEROUS DISCOVERY	*Laura Martin*	
THE UNEXPECTED LANDLORD	*Leigh Michaels*	

If you would like to order these books in addition to your regular subscription from Mills & Boon Reader Service please send £1.90 per title to: Mills & Boon Reader Service, Freepost, P.O. Box 236, Croydon, Surrey, CR9 9EL, quote your Subscriber No:................................... (if applicable) and complete the name and address details below. Alternatively, these books are available from many local Newsagents including W H Smith, J Menzies, Martins and other paperback stockists from 13 January 1995.

Name:...
Address:...
...................................Post Code:........................

To Retailer: If you would like to stock M&B books please contact your regular book/magazine wholesaler for details.

You may be mailed with offers from other reputable companies as a result of this application. If you would rather not take advantage of these opportunities please tick box. ☐